DEDICATION

I would like to dedicate this book to the Lord in hopes
that one person gets saved by reading it.

CONTENTS

ACKNOWLEDGMENTS

I would like to thank all of my family and friends for the patience God has granted them as I wrote this book. First I would like to thank my beloved 6th Grade English teacher, Hallie Hurst. She gladly gave up her time to closely edit and revise my story. Thank you so much for your patience and wisdom. I would like to thank Rose Mary Tomblyn for taking the cover picture. Your photography skills are greatly appreciated. In addition, I would like to thank Sarah Tomblyn for allowing me to use her horse, Xander. Thanks Xander for be so corporative with me for the picture. I also have a special thanks to my grandparents, Nelson and Joyce Lough. Thank you so much for you contribution to help me publish this book. I love you two so much! You are an extraordinary couple!

Next I would like to thank my mother, Rena Gillespie. Thank you so much for also proof reading my story and encouraging me to strive and do my best. You are my true friend, and I will always love you. I would like to send my love and thanks to my father, Matthew Gillespie, for his endless love and support. I would like to send a special thanks to Nathan Gillespie, my older brother, and Les Shreve for helping me format this book. Without them I would not have been able to finish it.

Thanks again to all my friends and family for your support and guidance along my journey. I would like to thank my readers for taking the time to read my book and hopefully enjoy it. Most importantly, I would like to thank the Lord for His guidance and wisdom, to help me write this book. I pray that through this book one person will be saved and realize the true meaning of life.

Sarah Gillespie

CHAPTER 1 MISSING

I sat motionless in the dark, staring at the floor. Why would he do that? How could he do that to her...to me? My mom sat weeping in the corner of our floor. How could her husband, my dad, do such a thing? I tiptoed to the back porch and stared at the full moon, thinking about him. He was a muscular man with curly brown hair and tender eyes. It felt like just yesterday when he carried me across our fields to the barn. He showed me the creek filled with gurgling sounds, our barn filled with the sweet horse and cow aroma, and he pushed me in that big squeaky tire swing. I remembered the way he looked at my mom with those big kind eyes. He loved her so. Now it was 10 years later, and here I sat on the porch swing at 16 years old in shock. I retraced my thoughts to the beginning.

 I awoke this morning feeling excited. It was my sixteenth birthday. My dad and I had big plans. He took off work, at Phil's Lumber Company, just so we could spend the day together. We were going to go on a horse ride on the trail like we used to when I was young. Then we were going to go fishing and have a picnic at our pond.

"Mom, what's for breakfast?" I called down the stairs. There was no reply. I sprinted downstairs still in my pajamas and was surprised to find a note on the table. The note said:

Dear Jess,

Your father hasn't arrived from the barn for his breakfast. I went to get him. I'll be right back.

Love,

Mom

I wasn't surprised. My father was often late for breakfast, because he enjoyed caring for our farm animals so much. I yawned while I walked up the stairs. I was going to put on my favorite outfit; my mom had gotten it for me for my birthday yesterday. It was a new pair of genuine leather boots and a matching vest with pale pink embroidery. I put on a comfortable pair of jeans for it was a cool Montana summer day. Then I put on an old pale pink blouse, and slipped on the vest. I grabbed one of my straw cowgirl hats off the wall peg. I tugged my boots on and was downstairs in a split second.

I wolfed down a plate of cold eggs and bacon my mom had made that morning and washed it down with a tall glass of milk. I sometimes wondered if girls at school thought I was weird for having such a big appetite. It seemed as though I had no friends there that were girls anyway. My only friends are my animals, my dad, and of course, Jeremiah. My mom was more like an acquaintance. I began to waver; no we are friends- just not like dad and me. After I finished my breakfast, I decided I should go and see what was taking mom and dad so long, and besides, I had to go and see Faith this morning. An image of Faith's elegance popped in my mind, with her brown soft mane, long strong legs, and the white spot sparkling above her nose between her eyes. Faith is the best horse known to man. She wouldn't hurt a fly, unless I was in danger of course. I was so excited to see her that I began to run.

As soon as I entered the barn there was no sight of Mom. I found another note on Faith's stall. What's up with Mom and these notes? Why not just wait and talk to me in person? Oh well, I shrugged. I quickly unfolded the paper, then a sharp pain went into my heart. It said:

Dear beloved Jess,

I can't find your father. I know he's not at work or at the house. Maybe he didn't go to the barn this morning. He hasn't gone to town because his truck is still in the driveway. I'm beginning to worry. All I know is that I woke up this morning and he wasn't at my side. I'm headed to all of his favorite places in search for him. Stay at the barn or the house so I know you're safe.

Love,

Mom

I felt as though my legs were jello; I couldn't stand any longer. I fell on my knees and began to weep.

"Where could he be? He knew how important today was to me." I whined. I crawled to the lock of Faith's stall and unlocked it. I slipped in the stall and lay sobbing by my only true friend. After a good while of crying, I began to do the daily barn chores. Once I finally completed cleaning out the filthy stalls, I decided I would have a horse ride, even if Dad wasn't there. Mom's words slipped into my mind '*Stay at the barn or the house so I know you're safe.*' I ignored the thought and went on to saddle up Faith.

We rode up into the woods, witnessing all the glorious sights. The ponderosa pine smelled so citrusy, it made me feel as if I were somewhere special. I shut my eyes and visualized myself being in Florida; soaking in the hot sun, eating oranges, pretending there was no tomorrow. I would lie there hours on end wishing, waiting for something, as if things were different.

The thought about going home for lunch made my stomach churn. I was in no mood to eat cereal, for my mother would not prepare me a meal in her distressed state of mind. I continued on for what seemed like hours imagining Faith and me living in Florida. I was picturing what it would be like if Dad didn't come back. This wasn't like him. He's always told us where he was going so we would not worry. I couldn't imagine what it would be like without him. Would I be forced to work for the extra money? Would mom quit work and mope for the rest of my young life, forcing me to have to become the responsible adult? She wouldn't, would she? I pressed my swollen eyes into Faith's mane. It felt as if she was the answer to all my problems. I dug my face into her neck.

"Is this what it's going to be like for the rest of our lives? Or am I just over reacting? He's never liked us to fret about him. He's always told us where he intended to go, if he intended to go anywhere," I stroked Faith. "Ugh! I only wish I knew the answer."

She didn't answer. I was so strange. Talking to animals is never going to solve my troubles. I turned Faith around and guided her on the path from which we came. It was time to go home.

When I finally arrived home at 9:35 I found my mom in the corner weeping. I rushed to her side not knowing how much pain I must have caused. As soon as she saw me she clutched me tight in a hug making me feel as though I could no longer breathe.

"I couldn't find your dad." She mumbled.

My heart took a nose dive. "W-What?" I stuttered.

She nodded her head soberly.

A tear rolled down my cheek as I stood on the porch and concluded my thoughts. This was the worst birthday ever!

Sarah Gillespie

CHAPTER 2 THE SECRETS OUT

I rushed to fix my hair; for he would be here soon. I tiptoed down the stairs so mom wouldn't hear me. Then I peeked out the window.

"What's taking him? He's always here at 7:00 sharp." I murmured.

Every morning Jeremiah took his daily jog. I couldn't help gazing at his burly shirtless chest every day. No doubt he worked with weights or was in the barn many hours a day. There couldn't be an ounce of fat on him. He had warm, chocolate eyes and curly blonde hair that would make any girl drool in admiration. His adorable smile always brought a grin to my face.

Finally I saw him jogging confidently on the dirt road. I opened our squeaky front door. Oh, how I hated this door! I hope mom didn't hear it. I closed it quickly, for he was now in speaking distance.

"Morning." He called.

I couldn't help but stare at his eyes. I'd had a crush on Jeremiah since I was 14 years old, and yet he looked at me as though I was his little sister. What drew my attention to him anyway? Was it his muscular body or sweet caring smile? Maybe it was his tender, loving brown eyes.

"Great weather we're having," He said as he slowed down.

"Yes, but it's a bit chilly lately." I rubbed my arms.

At that moment I noticed he was carrying an oversized package. "Do you need help with that?"

"Nah, I got it. You got three letters and a package too."

I gently took the letters and package and set them on the wicker chair on the porch, "You didn't have to get the mail for us,"

"Well, I usually get our mail and take it to the house on the way home from my jog. I guess they sent this stuff to the wrong address. It says here, Josh Taylor," He turned around, began to jog again, and waved. "Sorry I've got to run off, but I've got a lot of running to do."

"Bye. Sorry about the trouble with the mail." I called.

"No big deal," He shouted.

I watched him for a long time as he continued to jog down our dirt road. Then I felt stupid because he probably thought I was obsessed with him or something. He was the only friend I had at school; at least I thought. He was far more popular than me. I thought of myself as the annoying, smart kid who got on everybody's nerves. The only time they liked me was when they needed help with school work or wanted an easy A. Sure, I talked to people at school and got along with them very well, I just didn't have any close friends. Dad is always at work so we're never together, and Mom is nice and all but she treats me like a daughter, not a friend, unlike Dad does. I picked up the letters and sat down on the wicker chair. No mail for me, just three bills and a package for Dad.

"Maybe I should open it for him since he decided to leave me on my birthday." I whispered sadly and agitatedly. I went inside, laid the bills on the table, and sneaked out the back door heading toward the barn.

I ran toward the barn clinging to the oversized box. I went up to the loft in the left corner and plopped myself on a bale of hay. Should I really open this? Would Dad want me to open it since he wasn't here? I tossed my conflicting thoughts aside and ripped it open. A tear started down my cheek. It was for me. It was my birthday present. He had gotten me exactly what I wanted. It was a gold heart shaped breast collar for Faith and a matching necklace for me. I told dad to get the string for my necklace in leather just like Faith's breast collar so Faith and I would match completely. I thought it was a dream that would never come true, and yet here I sat holding it in my hands. He must have special ordered it so the leather and gold were identical. Oh, how I wish I could thank him this second. I climbed down from the loft so I could try the breast collar out on Faith. It fit perfectly, just like my necklace did on me.

"I will cherish this forever whether Dad is here or not." I mumbled into the soft brown ear beside me. The friendly horse nodded her head up and down as though she agreed. I knew she had no idea what I was talking about, but it comforted me to think she did. I stroked Faith's soft mane.

"You're my best friend today, tomorrow, and forever." I whispered in her delicate ear.

Mom didn't like our farm animals. She thought they were all smelly rubbish. She especially didn't like Faith. For some strange reason Faith despised her. Every time Mom tried to help out with the animals, Faith always found a way to discourage her. Maybe Faith had a strange vibe about my mom. Once when I was 10, Dad

13

had to work double shifts, leaving Mom and me to help with the animals.

First when Mom tried to brush Faith, she kept kicking her hind legs like crazy. Then when my mom tried to brush Thunder, the horse in the stall right of Faith, Faith neighed and Thunder also went spastic. The only way mom can easily help out in the barn is to shovel the manure or clean away from the horses. I kissed Faith on the nose and headed straight for home.

"Good morning Jessica." Mom said sadly when I stepped inside the cold, gloomy kitchen.

I could tell as soon as I walked in that Mom had sobbed all night. There were black circles around her puffy pink eyes. The frown on her face had overtaken her. I had cried last night too, but not nearly as much. "Mom," I said, "Are we going to hire a search team?" I questioned.

"I was planning to call around for one." She replied.

"Good because I miss him very much."

"What's that necklace you're wearing?"

I turned my head so I wasn't facing her. I knew I had done something I wasn't supposed to and I had a hunch she knew too. I used the tip of my new boot to make little circles on the dirty floor. "Um…. I….uh….got it from…a box."

"What box?"

"A box from…..the….uh….mail".

"Was it addressed to you?"

"Ok, Ok! No!! It was for Dad, but I thought it would be ok if I opened it! I took the box to the loft and opened it! Then I figured out it was my birthday present from him!" I yelled hatefully with tears spilling out of my deep blue eyes.

"I didn't know you wanted a necklace for your birthday."

"It's a special necklace. I wanted a breast collar for Faith and a necklace that matched. He got exactly what I wanted." I whined with tears pouring out of my eyes.

"It's all right." Mom said with her voice quivering, "I miss him too. I'll find a search team."

We sat at the table for what seemed like an eternity.

Then Mom finally said, "I have to go and do some errands. Do you want to come?"

Really I wanted nothing to do with moving from the place I sat right now, but I figured it would be good for me to get out of the house. "Sure."

"Good. It will help us get our minds off of the whole situation. Let me get my purse and we'll be off. Go ahead to the truck ok?"

"Ok." I released a sigh as I plunked in the passenger seat of our black Toyota truck. This was Dad's truck. We had to use it because Mom's minivan was at the mechanics. It needed new tires. The old ones were dangerously worn out. I leaned my head against the driver's seat. It still had his sweet cologne aroma.

"What are you doing?" Mom asked as she hopped into the truck.

"Well....uh....I...was...uh...." I stammered as I found my place on the passenger's side of the vehicle.

"I love it too." She smiled sadly.

"What's the first stop?" I tried to say happily.

"We're going to Danielle's house." She said somewhat blissfully.

Danielle was my mom's best friend. She was also Jeremiah's mother and our closest neighbor who lived about one mile away. That's how I sort of became friends with Jeremiah. We've known each other since we were in diapers.

"Why are we doing there?" I questioned.

"Oh, Danielle needs to give me a few things, and we were going to visit awhile."

"Huhh," I grunted.

"What's wrong?"

"I don't mind going to Danielle's house and all, but when you talk to her it can last five minutes or five hours."

"It won't last very long, I promise." She squeezed my hand trying to give me reassurance, but it was no use to my aching heart.

When we pulled up to the house, Jeremiah was sitting on the porch. He must have finished his jog early today, since it was already 8:00. Mom parked the truck and hopped out. I looked in the mirror to be sure my hair looked ok. It didn't look fabulous, but it was acceptable.

"Are you coming?" Mom hollered from the porch.

I opened the truck door and slipped out. I quickly walked to her side. "I'm here."

"Alright, you two can talk awhile while I visit with Jeremiah's mom. Is that ok with you guys?" Mom said merrily.

I was glad she had cheered up a little, but I knew it was a cover for what she really felt. I wish I could pretend as well as her. "Ok with me." I said.

"It's ok with me too." Jeremiah answered.

"We'll be finished probably in an hour." Mom opened the screen door and shut it softly. She seemed very eager

18

to see Danielle. She hasn't seen her in a few weeks because we've been so busy.

"Do you want to go to our barn and see the foal?" Jeremiah asked interrupting my musings.

"I'd like that." I smiled, "I'd like that a lot."

"I think I'll get a drink first."

"Me too." We walked into the living room and were headed to the kitchen when we were halted by a terrible scene.

I hadn't wanted Jeremiah to know what was going on in my life, but it looked like he was going to find out.

"Mrs. Taylor! Destiny, are you ok?" Jeremiah asked my mother worriedly.

"Do you know why she's crying?" Danielle Foremen asked looking towards me, "All I did was ask her how Josh was doing."

A painful wail came from my mother's mouth. Jeremiah and Danielle were impatiently staring at me.

"Well?" Jeremiah asked.

"Yesterday, my birthday, my dad and I were going to have a big day. He had taken off work just for me. Well, when we woke up he wasn't there. Mom went to look in the barn, he wasn't there either. Then she looked at all his favorite places on our property where he relaxed, and still he wasn't there. He hasn't been home since. Mom said this morning that we were going to hire a search team." Tears were rolling out of my eyes as my mom bawled on. A look of concern appeared on Danielle's and Jeremiah's faces.

"Is there anything we can do to help?" Danielle said in a kind voice.

I shook my head gravely.

"Are you sure you looked all over your land?" Jeremiah questioned.

"I don't know. Mom told me to stay home while she searched." Of course I didn't, I thought.

Jeremiah looked toward Mom. "Did you, Destiny?"

"I'.....m....pretty...sure." Mom answered through her sobs.

I couldn't hold it in any longer. An impetuous rush of tears poured out like a summer thunder storm. I was surprised to feel Jeremiah giving me a gentle consoling hug. I felt so stupid; of course we were friends or he wouldn't care so much.

"We'll do anything we can to help." Danielle said.

"I just can't understand why he would do such a thing! He's never been like that!" Jeremiah said angrily stomping around the room.

"Calm down, you're only making matters worse." His mother hushed.

Mom's tears started to subside, but I knew the feeling sure hadn't. I wish Dad hadn't left like that. What worries me the most is the thought of what could have happened to him? Where could he be? Why was he

there? Was anybody with him? There were so many
questions, yet so little answers.

CHAPTER 3 OUR MISTY

I awoke the next morning feeling like I was missing something. I walked downstairs and was surprised to see a letter on the table. The note said:

Dear Jess,

I went to do more errands this morning and I figured you wouldn't want to come. I'll be back at noon with Subway sandwiches.

Love,

Mom

I released an enormous sigh. Looks like another dull day for me. I trudged back upstairs to my room. As I walked in the door, a weight settled upon me. I plopped myself on the bed and thought about what was going on

today. I knew the search team was coming at 1:00 o'
clock to look for Dad. That's about it. I stared at my
messy room. My sky blue walls were glowing in the
morning light while my pale pink and blue curtains were
flowing in the morning breeze. There were clothes all
over the floor hiding the sandy tan carpet. My closet was
overflowing with clothes that were too small. Mom and I
were going to clean it out, but since Dad left, we haven't
given it the time or the thought of day. I slowly made the
bed with my pink and blue comforter. Then I picked up
all the things on the floor and glanced at my closet. I
callously shook my head. I didn't have the heart to clean
any longer.

I slipped on an old t-shirt, pulled on a pair of jeans
covered with holes, and tied on a pair of worn out tennis
shoes. I pulled my light blonde hair up in a tousled bun. I
then glanced at the mirror with disappointment. My once
soft blue eyes were overcome with sadness, and my face
looked overly pale. I wiped a tear that appeared on my
face. I needed comfort, love, or any source of affection. I
was headed to the barn. I needed Faith.

I quickly began to saddle Faith. Jeremiah had unexpectedly invited me to his house yesterday, and nothing could stop me from venturing over. He said he was going to show me his horse's foal. This was no ordinary foal. It was bred from my dad's horse, Spirit, and one of Jeremiah's horses, Chestnut. Chestnut and Spirit were both Mustangs. They both were a warm brown color with black, honest eyes. Spirit was especially beautiful, and Dad had trained him exactly what to do and when to do it. Chestnut was a great and friendly horse over all, but when you got on her nerves she could be very temperamental. Usually when the parent of a horse has a good disposition, the baby does too, so this foal should be a friendly, wonderful horse.

Jeremiah's a good horse trainer, but I believe Dad and I could easily out train a foal in comparison. Jeremiah and I were both 8 years old when we got our first horse. Faith was mine; his was Hercules. They were both quarter horses from two great horse owners. Without a doubt, I trained Faith much better. Faith is calm and sweet towards everyone, except Mom. On the other hand, Hercules is a well-trained horse, but can get very testy towards little things that Faith ignores. When a new horse comes into Jeremiah's barn, Hercules becomes confused or irritated, but Faith treats them as though she's known them her whole life.

"Let's go Faith." I said while rubbing her back sweetly. I led Faith out of the barn and into one of our unfenced fields. I stroked her mane, and in one quick motion, I hopped on her back and was off to Jeremiah's house. We took the short cut, because I was so very excited to see Jeremiah. *"Stop thinking such silly thoughts. He only likes you as a friend. You might as well accept it. He will never like a girl like you."* I told myself.

I stared off into our vast, green pastures. I soaked in the delicious smells of our land and smiled. No place held such majestic beauty that made a person's heart fill with pride.

Faith trotted through the green woods of budded black cottonwood and reddish purple western hemlock. The birds rejoiced and sang merrily along the ride. For one short moment, I began to feel as though dad was trotting by my side on Spirit. As if everything was back to normal. I shut my eyes and went back to a time when everything was bright and magical:

"Go, Faith, go!!" I jabbed my heels into Faith's gut.

"Jess, you don't have a chance!" Dad shouted.

"Just wait and see! Your Spirit is nothing compared to my Faith!" I taunted him.

"You wish!" We raced through a small valley separating two mountains.

"Just because you turned thirteen now and you're a teenager doesn't mean you can out ride me!" Dad bellowed as the horse gained speed behind me.

"Whatever!" I echoed into the mountains. I leaned close to Faith and whispered, "You can do this, we can beat him."

We continued on until we came close to the finish line, which was a small creek near the end of the valley. I dug my feet into Faith and shouted, "Go, Girl, go!!" I was almost there, only 20 yards away, with Dad right on my tail. Then SPLASH!! Faith practically jumped in the creak. We were first, and that's all that mattered. "I thought you were going to beat me," I teased.

"Ahh, I let you win," Dad smirked, revealing his pearly, white teeth.

I returned the smile along with a bear hug, "I love you, Dad."

"I love you too."

I wiped my eyes and tried to cover my true feelings. I brought myself back to the present, since we had arrived at Jeremiah's house. I went into the barn and was pleasantly surprised to see Jeremiah petting the foal. I put Faith in an empty stall and practically ran towards the foal and Jeremiah. I self-consciously tousled my hair hoping it looked decent. My eyes were locked on Jeremiah. When he looked in my direction, I panicked and quickly looked away, forcing them to the baby horse.

"Isn't she beautiful?" Jeremiah said in his dreamy voice.

I tried to keep my eyes glued on the animal in hopes he didn't notice my embarrassment. She was a prettier, richer brown than Chestnut or Spirit. She had big curious black eyes that looked at Jeremiah. "Yeah." I whispered. I sat down beside the foal and stroked her ever so sweetly. "What day was she born again?" I asked.

"I think it was a week ago."

"Oh, yeah I remember now." I had visited the foal countless times; she just never seemed so stunning before.

"I was hoping we could name her today."

A smile spread across my face. That was one of my favorite parts about horses, the name. "Umm.........Maybe we could name her..."

"Why don't we name her Misty?" Jeremiah said interrupting my verbal musings.

It was perfect. It was just right for her innocent and tender face. "I love it. I think it is the perfect name, Jeremiah."

"I thought you would think so," he said in that deep, melodic voice. "Do you want to come over for lunch? My mom's making lasagna and garlic bread."

"That sounds delicious. Good thing you invited me because my mom left this morning for town, and I was going to eat…….."

"Eat what? Is something wrong?" A look of concern spread over his face as he continued to stroke the foal behind the ear.

"What time is it?" I said wishing this moment would never end.

"Uhhhhhh….11:45, why?"

"Man." I mumbled to myself. I just lost my chance to eat with him. I have to go and eat dumb sub sandwiches with Mom.

"What did you say?"

"I can't," I said sorrowfully. "My mom's coming home at noon and she's bringing sub sandwiches. Sorry, maybe another time."

"What about dinner? Then you and Destiny can come."

"I can't do that either. The search team is coming at one. I don't know why Mom's leaving me at home. Mom said I can't help them look for Dad, so I will just be at home alone all afternoon and this evening worrying."

"I'm sorry."

"It's ok," Even though it wasn't.

"Is there anything I can...."

"No," I said a little too grimly interrupting him. "There's nothing that can be said or done to make this be better. What am I supposed to do? Use magic and make him reappear?"

I could feel the tears forming.

"No," He said benevolently. "You can pray. Do you want me to pray with you before you go?"

"Humph! This is all God's fault! Why would I want to beg and plead for Him to give back something He took away from me? This is all his fault!!!!!"

"Because God knows what's best in the long run. And..."

"I can't listen to your fairy fluff God. I have to go endure *real* life problems in the *real* world." I spun around with tears spilling out of my eyes, consequently leaving what pride I had in the barn. I took one last glance at Jeremiah's sympathetic, concerned face and I was gone.

When I returned home I was relieved to find that Mom wasn't home yet. After I put Faith away, I ran inside the house and acted as though nothing had happened while she was out. In about 10 minutes Mom came inside carrying tons of grocery bags. I ran to her side and took over half of the load.

"Thanks honey." She forced a smile. "There's more stuff in the truck. Will you go get it? I'll unpack the bags and put the things away."

I inched out the door and headed to the truck. How much stuff did the woman buy? I noticed that the truck was pretty full. I grunted, knowing this would take a while. She only went shopping about every two weeks, and when she did she meant business.

As soon as I grabbed the last package from the black truck, two linen white vans pulled into the driveway.

"Is this Destiny Taylor's home?" a tall red headed fellow asked as he and another man stepped out of one of the vans. "Are you searching for Joshua Taylor?"

I swallowed around a huge lump in my throat. "Yes," I whispered clutching the grocery bags tightly.

"Is your mother here?" A third man with bleached blonde hair asked as he stepped out of the second van. The last of the four men walked around the van carrying what seemed to be paper work. He nodded in agreement, that they needed my mother.

"Yes, I'll get her." I rushed inside and found mom putting cookies in the oven. "Mom, what are you doing?"

"Well, I just thought those helpful searchers deserved some cookies after they find Josh, I mean your father," she said gleefully.

"Mom, what if they don't find him?"

"That's ridiculous, of course they will! They are professionals you know."

"They're outside, and they want to speak with you." I grumbled.

"I'd better go. You stay here, understand?"

"Yeah. Yeah." I had a bad feeling about this. My stomach churned and my head seemed to spin. For some strange reason, I felt as though every bone in my body was achy, but I knew it was all in my head. I thought negatively too often, but this time I just knew it wasn't going to turn out well.

"Jess!"

"What Mom?" I walked onto our freshly painted white porch and hopped down the stairs where Mom stood.

"I'm going with these four gentlemen to assist them." She lowered her voice. "Take the cookies out of the oven, put the rest of the groceries away, and clean the kitchen."

I was about to say something in my defense on why I shouldn't have to clean the kitchen when she cut me off.

"I'm not in the mood for complaining, just do it. Be back soon, I hope."

If Dad were here he would have helped me clean the kitchen and made it fun. Once we had a water fight while Mom was at the store, and we were supposed to clean the kitchen. We still cleaned it and Mom never found out until she discovered water damage on the ceiling two weeks later. We were hoping she wouldn't look up. Another time we had a food fight before dinner when she went to buy more milk. It was lasagna night, and when Mom came home she about strangled us. The lasagna was everywhere. It was on the cabinets, the sink, my hair, and all over the floor. It probably didn't help that Dad and I had a lasagna skating race across the floor. We accidentally threw it on the ceiling too. The lasagna stain is next to the water damage. Every time I looked up I burst out laughing, until now. Now when I looked up, I burst into tears. Oh, how I longed to see his face. His smile could warm up the dreariest of days.

"Stop thinking about this! You're tearing yourself apart. Think positively," I whimpered. "I can't think positively! They're never going to find him!" At this point

I was on the floor curled up in a ball. "Why?" I screamed. Maybe I was working myself up. Maybe they would find him. But what did I know? I laid there for an endless time, my mind blank. I rested my eyes for a minute to see if I'd wake up from this nightmare.

Beeeep!! Beeep!! My eyes flew open. What? The smell of burning cookies told me this *was* a nightmare and that Mom would be disappointed.

"They were going to taste bad anyway!" I reassured myself. I picked myself up and began to clean the kitchen after I took the over baked cookies out of the oven. Suddenly I saw my reflection on a spoon. I looked a wreck. My light, blue eyes were puffy and pink. A huge frown shone intensely on my pale freckled face, and my dirty, blonde hair was a rat's nest. "Maybe I can take a shower after I clean this room." I rushed to finish cleaning and sprinted upstairs to take a shower.

When I was finished and started down the stairs I heard something. It was a small whimper. Was mom home? Was she crying? I tiptoed down the stairs to find out. It was coming from the closet. "That's strange," I thought, "Nothing important is in there." I was surprised to find an old battery toy dog whining. It wouldn't stop. I was about to throw it in anger when I realized dad had gotten it for me. I studied the small stuffed toy. It was a white dog with black spots. It was quite shabby and worn out. I took out the batteries and placed the toy back in its original box with the batteries at its side. I brushed my hand against its soft fur. I quickly turned away, forcing myself to look elsewhere. I leaned my head on the wall for support. I slowly began to sink to the floor; I could feel the storm coming. From anger and sadness, I dashed for the barn to Faith.

Sarah Gillespie

.

CHAPTER 4 MY WHISTLE

I rushed to get Faith's brush, since brushing her soft mane soothed me. I grabbed the brush from the shelf in the storage area and a fresh sugar cube. I went to Faith's side and brushed her warm, chocolate brown mane. I leaned against her head to sustain my achy body. She smelled of fresh hay. I soaked up the sweet fragrance. I closed my eyes and pictured myself riding on her with my hair blowing in the wind, smiling from ear to ear. I gently put the sweet treat to her fuzzy nose. She hastily licked the treat off my sweaty palm. I was so nervous. They could look all they want, they won't find him. I had a feeling in my heart that the search wouldn't succeed.

"Hello! Anyone in here?"

Jeremiah's voiced caused my eyes to fly open. "I'm in here. Do you need something?" I said as my heart skipped a beat and I popped my head out of the stall.

"I felt terrible for you. I thought since you would be home by yourself worrying, the least I could do was help with the chores in the barn. I figured there would be more work since Josh wasn't here."

My heart stopped. He was so compassionate. He was willing to help us in our time of need. I was a little offended that he thought I couldn't do the chores though. "Well, I can do it, but if you insist." I hurried out of Faith's stall and rushed toward Jeremiah practically running into him.

"I'll start cleaning out the horse stalls," he suggested.

"Ok," I said. "I'll brush the horses and feed them." We worked in silence for the longest time.

"Are you excited for school starting next month?" He finally asked.

I had forgotten about school. I kind of blocked it out. I hated it. I felt so out of place. I'd rather be here with Faith riding through the woods and exploring the world.

"Jess, did you hear me?"

"What?" I had forgotten I didn't respond, "Oh, I don't know. I'd rather have summer all year round and stay with the horses."

"I sometimes think that, but I like school, especially Alex."

I was sure glad I wasn't facing Jeremiah. I could feel the blood creeping up my face in rage. I didn't know he liked Alexis Bean. Once, she acted really nice towards me and paired up with me for a lab in science. Later that day, I overheard her talking to the other girls saying "I only paired up with her so I could get a guaranteed A+." They had all pointed and laughed arrogantly. She then made some rude comment about my hair and all the other girls giggled. My eyes stung. Jeremiah and I were meant to be together, not he and Alex.

"So you like Alex?" I asked.

"Yea, I love her bubbly personality."

"Yeah, she has a nice personality," I grumbled.

"What was that?"

"Nothing," Ugh, the girl was extremely cocky and condescending. She never had a curl on her head out of place. I could feel my fists tighten around the brush I was holding. I noticed I had begun to brush the horse with too much effort, causing him discomfort. I instantly pet the spot.

"Are you interested in anybody?" He asked as he went into the last dirty horse stall and I poured the last bucket of water for the horses.

I felt the heat rise to my face like fire. "Uh…. Nope." I hoped he'd accepted that lie. I wasn't about to admit my feelings for him. I couldn't, with the pretty Alex in the picture. I glanced at Jeremiah. He didn't even look up from digging out the stall. Figures, he could care less about me.

"Well I'd best be going back to the house."

"Ok. Thank you so much for helping me. You made a long job much shorter." I said with much gratitude. I could feel a heavy weight fall on me at the thought of Jeremiah giving Alex flirtatious smiles, the ones I've only dreamed of.

"No problem. See you later."

As I heard the barn door click behind him a tear rolled down my cheek. I trudged out of the barn and sprinted away from it all. I headed for the front of the house. A brief walk down the dirty road would surely help ease my pain, but I was halted by a strange scene in the yard.

The white vans were parked in front of the house and two searchers were talking to my mom with sober expressions. It looked as though the search had failed. I ran to Mom's side noting a huge frown on her face.

"I'm sorry ma'am." The bleach blonde man said. "The helicopters are on their way."

What? Helicopters?! No, it can't be true!

Mom nodded her head gravely in my direction.

"We saw absolutely no evidence of him," The red headed man said solemnly looking at me. "So we're sending in the helicopters. If the helicopters and other crew can't find him we don't know what else to tell you."

I stood still as glass, as if anyone touched me, I would shatter. My prediction was sorrowfully correct when I had hoped I was wrong. Mom looked at me hard then gave me a bear hug.

"Do you have the cookies?" She whispered. "I could use them right now."

I slowly shook my head. "I burned them," I swallowed down a big gulp of air. "Sorry."

"It's all right." She said as she stroked my hair in a motherly fashion.

"Did you look everywhere, mom?"

"Yes. We looked at all his favorite places and more."

"Mom, I had a feeling we wouldn't find him."

The red head man jumped into the conversation. "We never said we wouldn't find him, we just said we haven't found him."

"I know," I shuddered. "But I have this strange feeling you won't find him."

"Don't be so negative." Mom said with a little hope in her voice.

"The helicopters will be here at 4 o'clock. We are going to go pick up some other searchers," one of the searchers replied in a very serious tone.

Mom nodded. "Thanks for all your help."

The bleach blonde man waved and they drove off. I glanced at my watch. Three o'clock.

Mom stepped toward me slowly. "Honey, why don't we eat some cherry chocolate chunk ice cream?"

The words made my mouth water. That was my favorite ice cream and Mom didn't offer to buy it very often. "Yeah, ok."

"Maybe it will help." Mom responded trying to smile.

As we walked toward the truck, I did something I didn't do very often; I shut my eyes and said a little prayer.

Lord, I don't know if I'm doing this right, but help the searchers find my dad.

45

The vans returned near 4:00 only this time there were more. There were three vans with four people in each while the back of the vans held equipment. The twelve people jumped out of the vans and began to prepare themselves for the search.

Mom ran to the red headed man and asked, "Where is the helicopter and how long will it take for you to get ready?"

"Ma'am, the helicopter is coming and it will only take five minutes. You must calm down or you'll only make matters worse."

She nodded, while a tear rolled down her cheek.

I jogged to her side and asked, "Am I staying here again?"

She nodded again. "I'd prefer it. I don't want the chance of losing you too." She took a short breath. "I want to go and help as much as possible," she lisped, choking on her words. I could tell she was trying her best to be strong and optimistic for me.

I gave her a long hug. She loved my dad so much. My dad was lucky to have someone as beautiful as her who truly loves him. She had light blonde hair and deep green eyes. Her skin was as flawless as a model's, and when she smiled, the whole room lit up.

"Go inside," Mom said, interrupting my thoughts.

I ran inside and hopped on the maroon couch to peek out the window. Mom stepped in the linen van and they drove off. I sat on the couch staring at the fireplace for a long time, listening to the crackle and watching its sparkling glow. Then I quickly got up and ran to the barn.

The chores were already finished, so I decided to secretly go on a horse ride. "I'll just go to the fields and back," I told myself. I saddled Faith with her heart shaped breast collar, a saddle, and reins. Next, I put my helmet on and finally convinced myself to take the heavy first aid kit. I threw the first aid kit over the saddle and guided Faith out of her stall. When we were outside I could tell Faith was excited; she knew she was in for a fun adventure. I leaped on her back and we were off to the tire swing in the field.

The leaves were beginning to change their colors from crisp green to soft yellow. I soaked in the smell of autumn in the air. I smelled the fresh leaves, and just the thought of Thanksgiving made my nose imagine the sweet smells of pumpkin spice and cinnamon. It was my favorite time of the year, except for school starting, of course. I dug my feet into Faith's stomach telling her to go faster. I turned, faced the woods and looked at the orange and yellow trees. They looked so elegant and soothing. I bounced up and down as I told Faith to go faster. We took a sharp turn and I pulled Faith to an abrupt stop.

"We're here!" I announced as I patted Faith in a motherly fashion.

Faith trotted toward the lonesome tree in the middle of the field. I slid off her back and tied her to the dark tree trunk. I stroked her nose and kissed it. I reached in my pocket to retrieve a hidden sugar cube for her. She quickly slurped it off my hand and licked her lips. I walked over to the tire swing and sat down. I began to swing higher and higher. The wind blew in my face as I looked at my surroundings. I had the comfort of Faith being beside me to help take the horrendous pain away. I soaked in this magnificent moment; the birds fluttering around me, the swing squeaking loudly, and the sight of all the woods in the distance. As I went higher, it was all so calming and relaxing. I looked at my watch. 6'o clock!! Mom could be home soon.

I leaped off the swing and clambered on Faith's back. I dug almost as hard as I could into her sides with my heels alerting her to go as fast as she was able. She immediately obeyed the command and began to gallop. She was going so fast I couldn't see the world around me. I tried pulling on her reins so she would slow down. Something was wrong. She had never gone this fast before. Something was scaring her, but what? I could feel myself losing my balance. I began to lose grip of the reins, then the world went black around me.

Slowly my eyes opened, and I spotted Faith next to a tree munching on some grass. My head ached. What had happened? I remember riding, then falling. I must have hit my head and passed out or something. What time was it? The sun had gone down a little, but I could still see. My arms and legs seemed numb. My first aid kit was no use now, except maybe for the scrapes and cuts on my arms. I looked at my arm and it was bleeding excessively. Where did I fall? So many questions remained unanswered. I looked around and saw a large rock with blood on it. That wasn't a good sign. I was in a small ditch on top of some leaves. I whistled for Faith to lie down beside me, so I could retrieve the medical kit. I took the first aid kit off her back and began to dig through it. Good, hydrogen peroxide. I found a cotton swab and soaked it in the liquid. I placed it on the wound and I began to feel the pain. "Help!" I yelled with what little strength I had left.

I lay there helpless for a minute then started to search through the kit again. I found a bandage and stuck it on the cut. I knew there was a whistle in here that dad had told me about. He said if you were ever in danger, blow the whistle as loud as you can and stay put. I looked faster, I knew if I lost too much blood I may not make it. My bandage was soaked and dripping now. I began to panic. I grabbed several bandages and placed them on the wound, I grimaced at the awful pain. I saw something gleaming in the light. It was the whistle. I grabbed it and blew as loud as I could. While I was blowing, my mind started swirling and Faith became a blur. Then, once again, everything went dark.

"Will she be all right doctor?" I heard a voice question.

"Yes, but she needs to stay here a few days so we can run more tests to be sure."

"Thank you."

I could hear Mom's voice, but I could see nothing. I opened my eyes and gazed up at her. The doctor, at this time, had already left the room. "What happened?"

"We were looking for your dad when we heard this loud whistle and we rushed to the noise. We were surprised to see you though. You were lying on the ground unconscious. You must have fallen off Faith because she was nearby."

It was all coming back to me. "I....I....remember."

"What happened?" Mom asked with an obvious look of concern.

"I snuck out to ride Faith to the tire swing." I glanced up at her as though I knew she was mad at me.

Mom nodded, indicating to go on.

"After I swung awhile I realized it was getting late. I started riding home and Faith started going faster than usual. I lost grip of her reins and that's all I remember. Oh, except I woke up, put hydrogen peroxide on my cut, and blew the whistle. That's all I remember."

Mom nodded. "You shouldn't have left the house-"

"I know." I said shamefully interrupting her.

"It doesn't matter now," She said staring into my eyes mournfully. "They never found your dad."

I glared at the floor, and then I threw the apple from my lunch tray onto the floor. "Why Mom?! Why?"

"I don't know honey but getting mad won't fix anything. We're just going to have to accept the facts."

I grunted agitatedly. "No, but getting mad will make me feel better." I mumbled.

"Maybe so, but it's not right." The kindness in my mother's eyes left. Anger and hate soon filled them. "Danielle is all for this whole God thing. I've tried praying, and it doesn't work. All it does is give you false hope." She rolled her eyes, "I think it's all just a bunch of hogwash ."

My jaw felt firm. I nodded in agreement. "I've prayed to this God, and what does He do? Allow Faith to ride faster than usual from something scaring her, so I could end up in the hospital? Just what we need. More bills!"

When Mom was just was about to add to our conversation, Jeremiah and Danielle walked in the room, disrupting our discussion with blissful smiles.

"How are you feeling?" Danielle asked with huge eyes.

"I'mmm.....ok, I guess."

"We brought you these caramel chocolate kisses." Jeremiah said sympathetically. "We knew they were your favorite."

"Thank you." I said forcing a smile.

"What happened?" Danielle asked.

I gave mom's jacket a tug, indicating her to lean over closer to my face. "Will you make them leave?" I whispered. "I'm kind of tired and I want to rest."

Mom gave me a quick nod and led Danielle and Jeremiah out of the room. She closed the door behind her allowing me to have my privacy. I released an enormous sigh. Why all at once? Why must this all happen right now? I forced my head against the pillow trying to go to sleep. I closed my eyes picturing my life years ago, months ago, and days ago. Finally, I began to fall asleep dreaming of my simple life in the past.

CHAPTER 5 FINDING DAD

Squeak! Squeak! My tire swing swung back and forth.

"Jess! Jess!" it wailed.

It sounded like dad; it had to be dad. I flew off the tire and began galloping on Faith toward the noise.

"Jess! Jess! I need you!!"

There it was again. My head began to spin with all of the emotions. "Where are you, Dad?! I hear you!" I sobbed. The voice began to fade in the distance. An image of Dad popped into my confounded mind, then just as quickly it vanished. "Wait, Dad, wait!! Don't go!!"

My eyes popped open. I wiped the perspiration off my forehead. I clenched my sheets tightly, turning my knuckles white. I looked around; I was still in the hospital.

Mom was sitting in the corner reading *Better Homes and Garden.*

"Are you all right, honey? You look disturbed."

"Uh.......I just had a weird dream is all."

"Well, ok. Why don't you eat your dinner before it gets cold? The mashed potatoes are to die for."

"I'm not all that hungry."

"Well, you better eat up so you can regain your strength."

"Ok." I replied anxiously.

"Haaa!! Haaa!!" I giggled when Dad tickled me.

"Today my daughter turns 4 years old, which means she's not afraid of the tickle monster."

"I never said that." I laughed.

"Here I come to tickle you," he said in his monstrous voice.

"You'll never catch me." I squealed.

"Oh yeah!?"

All of a sudden he began to fall, as if he was in horrendous pain. "Jess. Jess." He whimpered.

"What Dad, what?" I screamed.

I rolled off my bed, dropping onto the floor. "Oww." I mumbled. Why do I keep having these dreams? I keep having this feeling he's still alive.

"Honey, are you ok? I heard a loud thud."

"I'm ok. I just keep having these weird dreams about Dad."

"Well, honey, now that you're fully recovered from your fall I thought I should tell you this.

"What?" I whispered.

"The searchers continued looking for your dad and they confirmed that your father isn't alive."

I felt as though I had been kicked in the gut. "It's not true!!" I hissed, "I know he's alive, they must not have looked hard enough!"

"Honey," Mom cradled me in her arms as I began to sob, "He's not coming back, he's gone. They didn't find a trace of him."

I pulled free from her clutches, tumbling onto the floor. I snatched my blue, fuzzy robe from the peg and stomped downstairs.

"Where are you going?" she pleaded.

"To get breakfast!" I huffed.

She was at the top of the stairs now looking at me as though she could cry. "Are you going to be all right?"

"I'll be fine." I grunted while stuffing a chocolate chip muffin in my mouth and gulping it down with some fresh milk.

"I'm going to go take a shower. Then I'm going to call the hospital, and try to get a full time job."

"Ok." I had forgotten about that. Dad provided us most of our money, so now Mom had to get a full time job. I heard the shower turn on. Now Mom would have to work all day instead of being a part time nurse. I put my cup in the sink. I knew Mom was wrong about Dad and I was going prove it!

It was dark and the moon light shone brightly. "I'm doing it tonight." I whispered. **I tiptoed out of bed and put on my old clothes then tugged on my worn out boots. I had written a list last night, now where was it? Ahhh, there it is!**

List to Find Dad

1. Get dressed
2. Pack extra outfit and shoes
3. Pack plenty of food for up to a week
4. Write note to Mom
5. Sneak outside to barn
6. Pack first aid kit
7. Saddle Faith and hitch extra supplies

8. FIND DAD

Ok, I did number one. Check. I picked up a small, brown duffle bag and placed one shirt, two jeans, a sweat shirt, a small jacket, and a few pairs of socks and underwear. Then I scurried downstairs with my things and a bag for the food. I put canned beans, canned potatoes, canned meat, bread, a few apples, lots of frozen water bottles, and a few bags of cereal. I put a can opener, a lighter to start fires with, a few utensils, and other necessities in another bag.

I grabbed a sheet of paper and began writing:

Dear Mom,

Don't worry about me. I'm off to search for Dad. I don't know when I'll be back, but I have enough food for a week. I will have my whistle to alert you if I'm in danger. I'll be taking Faith. Please don't bother looking for me, because I'm not willing to come home under these circumstances. I love you. Be home soon.

Tons of Love,

Jessica

I placed the pink letter on the table underneath a vase full of flowers. The vibrant slip of color peaked out from under it. There, how could she miss that when she's cleaning the table?

"Ok, number five," I told myself, "Wait I almost forgot a watch!"

I hurried upstairs and snatched my wrist watch. Then I practically sprinted through the darkness with my things to the barn.

When I got there, I looked at my watch. Ten till midnight. I lit a lantern and grabbed the first aid kit off the shelf. I hastily grabbed the lantern and brought it toward Faith's stall. "Hey, girl," I whispered rubbing her nose. I saddled her up and stuffed all the supplies in her saddlebags. I bundled a few extra things I had forgotten including a flashlight and other needed equipment into a blanket and tied it onto Faith behind the saddle. Finally, I grabbed Faith's mane and forced myself on her back. Soon we were gone in the darkness.

We rode in the darkness for a few hours. I clicked a button on my watch which caused the light to show, 3:00 A.M. Maybe we should make camp for the rest of the night. I stumbled upon a clearing where the moonlight shone around the area, making it appear quite cozy.

I climbed down from Faith. She looked at me as though she were in need of a good pet and a fresh sugar cube. Good thing I packed my pockets full. I dug in my pocket and pulled out a cube. Before I could lift up my hand to her nose it was gone, quickly melting in her mouth. I almost always felt as though there was a connection between us, like she knew what I was thinking and I knew what she was thinking. At this moment she seemed to feel pleasant and at ease. I reached over top of Faith and grabbed a blanket and my small pillow. Faith curled up on the ground, and I laid against her for protection and warmth. Before I knew it, I was fast asleep.

I woke up feeling achy to the bone. "Ohhh!" I groaned stretching my arms over my head. Faith was already up munching on the grass. I looked at my watch, which read 8:00. I walked over and picked up a can of beans out of my duffle bag on the ground where I had taken it off Faith for the night.

"How are you, Faith?" I asked stroking her back.

"Good, how are you?" she seemed to say.

"Yeah, me too, I'm feeling really energized."

I pulled the supplies off her back and began to make a fire and cook my beans.

After I had finished eating what I thought was a delicious meal, I began to pack my things for the journey ahead. I climbed up on Faith and put her in a trot.

"Where should we go?" I asked her.

Faith's head began bobbing up and down toward the east as if to say, "Let's start that way."

I nodded, "Good thinking, girl." I stroked her as we continued trotting, "We should go toward 'the rocks'. **Maybe Dad was planning a surprise there for me. Maybe he could have been planning out a rock climbing** adventure he had promised me some time ago." My **mind went back in time to** when I was twelve years old:

"Are you ready for that hiking trip?"

"You bet!" I bounced up and down. We were going to 'the rocks'. Dad had told me about it countless times. About its tall, fearful cliffs and amazing views. They weren't really what you call rocks, they were enormous mountains, but we called them rocks for short.

"Mom, are you coming?" I called in the barn.

"No, honey I've got housework to do," She walked over and gave me a gentle, light hug, "Have fun though."

"You're going to miss out on all the fun."

"I know. Now run along so you won't keep your dad waiting."

"Ok." I sprinted toward Dad standing next to the fence outside the barn, "Ready?"

"Yep, let's go."

I trotted upon my sweet, young horse, Faith. Smiling ear to ear I began to hum a simple tune.

"Sure is pretty out here, isn't it?"

"Yea," I whispered.

We rode in silence most of the way, enjoying all the sights and views.

"We're here!" Dad announced.

I gazed at the most beautiful sight I'd ever seen. There in front on me were five enormous mountains capped with snow. There was a gurgling creek a few yards away from me. There were also a few scattered elk in the distance.

Faith neighed as if to say, "Let's get started!"

I stroked her mane and whispered in her ear, "I can't wait either."

My eyes were still glued on the miraculous scene. There were trees as far as I could see and animals *everywhere I looked. Rabbits frolicked in the tall grasses. Birds, of all shapes and sizes, sang sweet melodies in search of their mates. Wild horses in the distance were chasing each other as if they were in a race and the other just had to win. I was mesmerized.*

"I love it, Dad."

"I thought you would," He smiled, his deep dimples showing, his eyes glowing with excitement.

"It's marvelous," my smile widened showing my deep dimples as well, "It's breath taking."

"All very true," he answered.

I closed my eyes thinking it was a dream, but when I opened them it was still there.

"Well, let's begin our hike."

"Finally!" Faith seemed to say as she neighed happily.

Starting our adventure, we rode through the grasses and the creek. We rode up the mountains as high as we could go looking down on the breathtaking landscape.

"These mountains are very steep," I commented.

"Yes, they are," he stared up at them, "Maybe someday, if your mom allows it, you and I can climb up them."

"Then we can sky dive down," I winked at him jokingly.

"Yeah, right like your mother would allow that!" he said sarcastically.

I laughed. "I know. We're lucky she let me go on this hike today."

"I know, I know," he said. He shook his head, with a grin.

I went to stroke Faith, when she began to act more vigorously. Something was wrong, but what?

All of a sudden a mountain lion screeched far in the distance.

Horror shone brightly on my face as I struggled to maintain control of Faith.

Faith tipped her head back and stood on her hind hooves. I grasped the reins as tight as I could, but my hands were beginning to slip. Faith was as close as she could get to the edge of the trail. One slip and we could fall to our deaths.

I began to panic, but I couldn't panic aloud for it would only make matters worse. She would then know it was most definitely a dangerous being. Luckily, dad's horse, Spirit, wasn't affected by the horrendous noise. Dad swiftly moved his muscular arms toward the reins and pulled Faith to an abrupt stop. As he jerked the reins her hooves slipped on the edge and we almost lost our balance.

I glanced below. The elks looked like ants, while the creek looked as though it were a crack in cement. The rocks beneath me were bigger than Faith. With their jagged edges and large form, we would have never made it without Dad.

Dad grabbed me in a bear hug, not wanting to release me from his arms. He placed a small kiss on my forehead, and said softly, "I love you more than you'll ever know,"

I wiped my eyes and held him tight. "Thank you," I murmured into his chest.

For the rest of the trip I stayed on the inside of the ledge. Dad whispered calm, sweet words in Faith's ear to keep her calm. She slowly began to settle and we decided we'd better head home. We trotted down the mountain.

Once at the bottom, we decided we should have a race home. I kicked Faith's stomach and screamed, "GO, girl!"

I galloped fast with the wind blowing in my hair. The familiar smell of pine tickled my nose. I barely beat him as I raced inside the barn and sat on a hay bale. Acting as though he had taken forever, I propped up my feet and locked my hands behind my head. We didn't get inside the house until almost midnight due to the long trip.

Suddenly I realized we had arrived at 'the rocks.' I squinted at the mountains trying to see if I could get a glimpse of him. Sadly, I saw nothing but a lone mountain goat. I sighed, feeling depressed. "Should we go up the mountains or look on level ground first?"

I decided that we shouldn't go up the mountain, because what if there was another mountain lion? Who knows what could happen then? "Let's look in the forest a ways." I told Faith, half hopeful, half depressed, and homesick already.

Faith, on the other hand, seemed full of happiness and ready for any obstacle to come. I wished I felt the same.

Destiny Taylor paced around the kitchen wondering what to do. "Where's my baby? Where's my baby? Maybe she's at Jeremiah Foremen's house checking on the foal."

Destiny picked up her phone and dialed their number.

A deep male voice answered, "Hello?"

"Jeremiah?"

"No, this is Brian Foremen."

"No time for chit chat, this is Destiny. Destiny Taylor, your neighbor. May I speak with Jeremiah or Danielle please?"

"Yes, of course Destiny. I'm sorry I didn't recognize your voice. "

"It's fine, please can I talk..."

"Yes, yes, I'll get Danielle."

After a couple of endless minutes a gentle feminine voice was on the phone. "Hello?"

"Is Jess there?"

"I don't believe so, but I'll ask Jeremiah,"

In the background of the phone she could hear Danielle's voice say, "Is Jess here?"

Sadly she heard the response as well, "No," Jeremiah answered, "Why?"

"I don't know, honey,"

Danielle returned to the phone, "No, why?"

Destiny could not hold it any longer, "I can't find her!" She wailed, "I looked all over our property, around the house and where she usually hangs out. She never goes far from home by herself."

"Did you see a note?"

She sniffled, "No."

"Maybe we should call the search team."

"I already have and they're booked all this week. By then, she'll be wolverine food."

"Jeremiah, Brian, and I can help you look for her, but we should probably start tomorrow because we might get lost in the dark. The sun's almost down."

"I guess." Destiny sniffled.

After listening to his mother's private conversation from another phone, Jeremiah was determined to make a plan. "I'll have to find her myself," he grunted. He'd become quite fond of Jess, even if she didn't know it. He'd recently liked Alexis Bean, but for some strange reason when he was around Jess he became more tongue tied every day. Maybe it was her spunky, outgoing personality. Or her sweet, blue eyes. Whatever it was, it was breath taking. An image of Alexis Bean popped in his mind. She had dark brown hair, with devious dark eyes he'd never noticed before. Then he thought of Jess. She had a genuine, caring disposition and heart- warming smile. He waved the thought of her in his arms out of his head. He was sure the feeling was not mutual. He began packing his things to set out on his journey to find Jessica that night.

Sarah Gillespie

CHAPTER 6 JEREMIAH'S PRIZE

"Darkness is falling quicker than I'd hoped," I told Faith. I dreaded the thought of sleeping on the cold, hard ground another night, but it wasn't like a bed was going to fall out of heaven. Then all of sudden, out of the blue, I said a small prayer again.

Dear Lord,

Please help keep me safe and watch over me. Amen.

Why did I do that? I rarely ever prayed. I used to not understand prayer; I still don't completely. Who taught me again? I remember, Jeremiah. Just the thought of his name warmed my heart. His brown eyes and sandy blonde hair popped into my mind. My heart ached to be home now, but it ached even more for the loss of Dad.

I remember when Jeremiah took me to church with him once. They had talked about a man named Jesus who had apparently died on a cross for my sins. It was all so very confusing. He took me there several times after that, but I still don't quite have a grasp on things. He'd taught me to pray while we were at church. He said, "Praying is really easy. You can say whatever you want. We can make it easier by starting with Dear Lord, saying what's on your mind, and ending with Amen."

My mom and dad had never taken me to church, except occasionally on Christmas and Easter. I never had really paid attention. I just liked watching the other children act out the plays. Jeremiah said it was important to know the Lord closely if you really wanted to live. Live? What did he mean by live? I patted my legs and waist. I seemed to be living. I shook my head in disgust and confusion.

I brought myself back to the present and began looking for a place to make camp for the night. "Faith, what about here?" I gestured in a sweeping motion as my other hand remained tight on her reins.

She immediately laid down on a small patch of grass surrounded by trees. I threw my head up and laughed merrily. I clamored off her back almost falling on the ground. I quickly began to pitch my tent, so I wouldn't feel as vulnerable. I attached my bag of food in between two, long ropes. I slung each end of the rope over two branches in two different trees. Next I laid a heavy rock on the remaining ends. Then I secured the rope on both ends very tightly on the ground, causing the bag to be in between two trees so no animals could reach it. I put the rest of my supplies in my tent and secured Faith to a tree with another long rope. I climbed in my tent, only to miss my fluffy bed. I laid my head on my lifeless pillow and huddled under my blanket. I released a small sigh, hoping sleep would come soon.

The wind was blowing rapidly in his face as he gained speed. Jeremiah began riding in the woods after he'd snuck out. He'd left a note explaining what he was doing, so he wouldn't ruffle his mother's feathers too much. Jeremiah patted Hercules on the neck and gave his mane a comforting rub. Jeremiah put Hercules at a slow trot when they reached the Taylor's barn. "Jess!" He called. No answer. What did Mrs. Taylor say? "I looked all over the property and in all her favorite places."

This is one of her favorite places, so she's probably not here. "I'm so stupid." He told himself, "We should try in the woods somewhere. I bet you a million dollars, she's out searching for her father getting into all sorts of trouble."

Jeremiah felt his heart lurch in complete terror. What if Jess went to the mountains and fell off a cliff? What if she encountered a mountain lion? So many thoughts swarmed through his mind concerning Jess. This can't be happening. He pinched himself hoping he somehow would wake up. Sadly his plan failed. He kicked his feet into Hercules' stomach, indicating that he go at a canter; he was headed for the mountains. Jeremiah began to pet the horse to placate himself as he rode.

"What am I going to do when I get there?" Jeremiah asked Hercules worriedly.

Hercules seemed content to be out of the barn and on an adventure.

"If you only knew what was really going on." Jeremiah patted Hercules. Jeremiah sighed. This was going to be a long ride alone in the darkness. Jeremiah shuddered at the thought of Hercules tripping in the darkness. Jeremiah sent up a little pray for guidance and wisdom. Thankfully the moon came into view from behind the clouds. Jeremiah sent a prayer of thanks for the extra light he had needed. Hercules was wrong; this wasn't going to be an adventure at all, more like an exhausting, dramatic experience.

The noises outside the tent deeply frightened me. A wolverine screeched in the distance. At that moment a realization hit me hard. I had forgotten a gun! I suddenly felt defenseless and alone. I shuddered at the thought of a wolf pack, a bear, a mountain lion, or anything else wandering into my campsite and killing Faith. What

would I do then? Climb up a tree and hope for the best?
I rolled over on my side.

"I have to be brave." I told myself. Maybe Jeremiah's
God was with me? Wait, this is all God's fault anyhow!
My luck he'll send a whole force of animals to come and
get me. Oh well, if I can't find Dad I'll have to die trying. I
gritted my teeth for determination, "I can do this." I told
myself. "I can!"

I wonder what Mom and Jeremiah are doing right now.
I wonder if Mom found my note. Either way she'd be
here soon in search for me. I sighed; I probably caused a
lot of trouble. They were probably looking for me this
minute and called the search team. I heard an owl nearby
on a tree. I huddled under my cover to ease the anxiety I
contained. I wish I were home. *No, you don't. You want
to find Dad.*

" Ahh," I massaged my temples. This was so
overwhelming. I bet I look a sight. How I longed for a hot
bath already. It hadn't even been 48 hours. I shut my
eyes yearning for rest. "Sleep," I groaned. I turned on my
side, staring at the strange shadows outside my tent. I
listened to the owl as it hooted victory in the meal he'd

just caught. If only I could find Dad as swiftly as that bird had caught its prey!

Jeremiah stopped Hercules to allow him to rest and to have a long drink. "There you go boy," he whispered, stroking the horse's neck. "Where are we now? I think we're a few miles away from the mountains. Should we keep going?"

Hercules laid down after munching on some grass, indicating he was quite finished for the day.

"Well, I'm kind of tired too," He grabbed his supplies from his saddle pack, "I'll start making camp." Jeremiah glanced at his watch, 3:00 A.M. "We'd better rest a few hours and start at day break."

Hercules responded by placing his head on the ground and shutting his eyes. He obviously was tired of the adventure already. Jeremiah decided he was too lazy to pitch his tent, so he grabbed his rifle and curled beside Hercules for warmth, with a pillow and a blanket.

Jeremiah awoke at 6:00. Something had awakened him. He looked around his small and defenseless campsite. Hercules was acting strange. He was already on his feet with his ears back, as if eavesdropping on an important conversation. His face looked vastly troubled and his eyes looked frightened.

Then Jeremiah saw it in the corner of his eye. It was an enormous grizzly. The bear had to weigh at least 1,400 pounds and stand on his hind legs at about eight feet tall. His claws looked to be about four inches long and his paws were easily as big as a magazine. Jeremiah blinked his eyes in amazement. Hercules was out of site now. Where had he gone? The bear walked toward Jeremiah on all fours, sniffing everything in his path.

"What if he eats my food, or what if I'm his food?" Jeremiah thought. The bear was at arms-length at that point and Jeremiah couldn't move. He didn't want to make any sudden movement. The bear had black, curious eyes and had blood stained fur around his mouth from his last meal. Jeremiah couldn't budge his arms to load the rifle. He began shaking when the bear trudged in front of him and stuck his wet nose in his face.

Jeremiah swallowed back a terrified scream. The monster seemed uninterested in him. The bear began to walk toward his supplies, so now was his chance. Jeremiah promptly loaded the gun. *Click.* The bear turned in his direction, but Jeremiah didn't budge. The bear began to rummage through Jeremiah's things once again. Jeremiah timidly aimed the gun to the bear's back. *BANG!! BANG!!* The bear turned toward Jeremiah and roared. His eye's no longer appeared curious for they were now cold and furious. He stood on his hind legs with his paws in the air shrieking at the pain in his back. The bear glued his eyes on Jeremiah as if to say you're dead. Jeremiah knew he couldn't out run him if he tried. Some grizzlies could run up to 35 miles per hour in short bursts. He aimed at the massive mammal a second time. *BANG!! BANG!!* The bear began running towards Jeremiah to gain his revenge.

"Lord, be with me please!" Jeremiah pleaded. He aimed a final time. *BANG!!* The bear dropped. Jeremiah ran toward his prize, but stayed a few yards away just in

case the bear was still alive. The bear wobbled up and clumsily walked toward him then fell flat on the ground. He did this a second and a third time, then fell a final time. Jeremiah released a relieved sigh.

"Thank you, Jesus!" He proclaimed. Jeremiah jumped for joy. He picked up the monsters rough paws and made them dance with him in excitement. "I did it! I did it!" Jeremiah chuckled at the thought of his mother's face when she heard the tale. Jeremiah pet and examined the animal. It was big all right!

"I wish I could take him home." Jeremiah said ruefully, "Now where did Hercules go? Hercules, here boy!" Jeremiah yelled.

Jeremiah called for his horse a couple more times. Then he heard hooves in the distance. It was Hercules running from the east.

"It's over, boy." Jeremiah whispered.

The horse nodded in reply.

"If only Jess was at my side and this was over, then I would declare this day great." Jeremiah told himself, "Thank you Jesus for letting us survive through this life threatening expedition. Thank you!" **Jeremiah walked toward his supplies while holding back thankful tears of** joy. "I wonder what Jess is doing right now?" Jeremiah **pondered as he began to examine his equipment.**

"Are you ready Faith?"

The horse neighed an ear piercing cry that could have been heard for miles; it was truly amazing.

"I thought so." I hopped on top the saddled mare and **jabbed my heels in her sides. She raced toward the river,** which was about 6 miles north. "Come on girl." I encouraged.

We rode in the silence, listening to the pleasant sounds around us. As we followed the Wise River, we listened to the birds humming their love songs and enjoyed the delicious smell and sound of the trees ruffling in the breeze. I soaked up the delightful aromas and sights. They were all so beautiful in their own way.

Once we finally reached the Big Hole River, I smiled at the miraculous scene before my eyes. The river had countless rocks peeking out of the sparkling water. The foliage around the river was blooming and I could see the fish popping out of the deep pool. I loved going fishing out here. Dad and I caught countless trout and bass in this gorgeous waterway. I inched Faith in the water and let her bend her head for a drink. I allowed myself to have a long swig of my water from my water bottle, for it was a hot Montana summer day.

"Dad!" I hollered. No answer. "Dad! Dad, where are you?!" Again no answer, all I could hear was the breeze and Faith cheerfully munching on grass. "Is that all you ever do, girl?" I patted the horse playfully.

She didn't seem to care. She was too intent in her meal to mind.

I wandered around the Big Hole River for hours searching for Dad. At lunch we decided to take a break. We found a bulky tree with the perfect amount of shade we needed.

I tied Faith to the shade tree, plopped myself down on the cool, hard ground and had a can of fruit for lunch. I began chomping on my meal, then Jeremiah appeared in my mind. *"God is great and God is good. And we thank Him for this food. By His hands must all be fed. Give us, Lord our daily bread. Amen."* Jeremiah's family had always sung that before they ate their family meals. Before I knew what I was doing, I was bowing my head and singing the prayer. Once I finished, I blinked my eyes in disbelief. *Why am I doing this? What is happening to me?* I shook my head in disbelief. Why do I keep talking to God when I know if it weren't for him, Dad would be home? For the rest of the meal I sat contemplating who and what this so called God really was and how he got here. *Was He on my side? I can't even see Him and He was going to help me? Why would He want to help me? Why would I want his so called help anyway?*

My brain was so perplexed. I gathered my equipment so I could continue the search, even if I was deeply bewildered.

Sarah Gillespie

CHAPTER 7 MY KNIGHT IN SHINING ARMOR

Once Jeremiah reached the mountains, a shiver went up his spine. He had pictured Jess on the mountains again, falling to her death. He swallowed back the horror.

"Jess!! Jess!! Where are you?" Jeremiah wailed. This was hopeless. Jeremiah cantered Hercules toward the mountains in the distance. She wouldn't be dumb enough to go up those would she? She was smarter than that. Jeremiah looked around all the areas where he thought she would be near the mountains. He released a depressing sigh.

"Jess! Jessica!?" He held the sob down in his throat. I wish she were here in my arms and we could go on home. Jeremiah shook away the comforting thought of having her cradled in his arms. Jeremiah trotted Hercules toward a blue, clear creek leading toward the Wise River. "Should I follow the creek toward the river?" He asked Hercules as the horse lowered his head for a long refreshing drink.

"I think we should" Jeremiah said to himself, "I have a strong feeling about going toward the Wise River and the Big Hole River."

Jeremiah soon began galloping toward both the rivers, somehow sure that Jess was in trouble.

As the evening sun began to fall, clouds found its place. I started to seek out a good campsite for the night. I found an area with a gorgeous view of the Big Hole River. *BANG! BOOM!* I glared up in fright and anger. It definitely was going to rain. I quickly began to pitch my tent. For tonight I would just have to put my food in the tent with me. No time to waste tying it up. A flash of lightening hit the sky. Faith shrieked in complete terror. I ran to her side and began to soothe her.

"It's ok girl." I pet her neck and mane.

I raced to finish pitching my tent, once I vigorously loosened Faith's saddle and threw it on the ground. After the tent was done with sturdy poles and some extra rocks inside, I threw the saddle in the tent with all my supplies. I tied Faith tightly to a strong tree and leaped inside the tent. As soon as I hit the ground buckets of rain poured down. A relieved sigh escaped my tired body. I sat in the dreary dark listening to the rain and poor Faith panicking outside.

"I'd let you in, if you could fit," I called to her.

Her response was more screams of fright.

"I'm sorry, girl," I yelled.

I lay down on the hard, cool ground. Just as I began to fall asleep, Faith made a different shriek. A shriek sounding like the thunder storm wasn't even there. It sounded more masculine than any of her shrieks. I sat up; maybe I should check on her. But then I'd get soaked in this freezing, cold rain. Just as I was about to unzip my tent and go in the rain, the lightning struck and I saw two four legged animals' shadows through my tent. One was definitely Faith; she seemed panicked with her ears back and as far away from the other animal as her rope would allow her.

Thunder rumbled across the sky, and then another lightning bolt struck. Then at that precise moment I knew what the animal was that slinking closer to Faith. It made a shrill cry verifying my knowledge. I didn't move a single muscle fearing that it might hear me. If Jeremiah's Lord was real, where was He now?

Once Jeremiah finally reached the Big Hole River, the rain was pouring so hard he could barely see. Hercules was nervous the whole ride over and was now in a panic, pulling at the reins. Jeremiah began to squint his eyes in an attempt to see farther than two feet in front of him. He could see that the river was rising rapidly.

"I hope Jess isn't camped close to the river." he told himself.

Lord, be with Jess wherever she may be.

At that moment the lightning struck, lighting up the whole sky with colors of yellow, orange, and pink. Then in one quick instant a tree before Jeremiah lit up in glowing flames. Hercules hurled back on his hind legs, almost causing Jeremiah to crash onto the ground behind him.

"Easy boy!" Jeremiah shouted in a soothing tone. The stud eased up a bit, but was still in a frenzy. The tree crashed onto the drenched ground blocking what little path they had before them. Jeremiah backed the horse up then pushed him into a full sprint. "We can do this boy!" Jeremiah coaxed. In one sudden jump Hercules leaped over the flames below him. Jeremiah pulled Hercules back into a canter and patted his neck. "That a boy!" He yelled through the thunder bellowing in the night sky.

"Please let me find her Lord," Jeremiah pleaded with God, *"I can't afford to lose my dear friend that may have even become a closer friend than that."*

I shut my eyes wishing this was a horrendous nightmare. Once I reopened them however, I was sadly mistaken. The mountain lion was slinking toward Faith inch by inch. Faith backed up as far as the rope would allow her to go. If only I hadn't tied her up. *If only that so called God were real.* I can't let my precious horse get torn to pieces before my very eyes. Impetuously, I unzipped the tent and crawled out. Then the mountain lion turned his attention to me.

"Please don't hurt me," I begged. Tears were spilling from my eyes and blurring my vision. A sob was stuck in my throat and was threatening to spill over in any instant.

In the distance, I could hear a faint *clip-clop, clip- clop* of a horse. "Jess! Jess!" The voice screeched.

I strained to speak, but only a squeak would come out. "I'm here," I tried to yell in my loudest voice. The mountain lion was inches away from me now and my heart just about stopped. It's breath smelled of death as it leaned closer to my face. The horse's beats drew closer and closer. As the lightning hit again across the sky, I could see that my rescuer was Jeremiah. He bounded off his horse, and rushed toward my side. The mountain lion looked him straight in the eye as if to say 'I'm not afraid of you!'

Jeremiah held a rifle in his hand and shouted, "Back away slowly from him. I'll try to lure him away from you and Faith." Jeremiah paced a few yards away still facing the cat as I tiptoed out of the scene. The mountain lion had his eyes glued on Jeremiah and looked as though he was ready to pounce at any moment. He moved toward Jeremiah slowly as Jeremiah walked little by little, farther away. I turned my head when he aimed his rifle and fired.

I glanced back at the scene. He'd done it! He'd killed the mountain lion and was my knight in shining armor.

Jeremiah couldn't help but smile until his lips hurt. He was so proud of himself for saving Jess. *When did I become so brave?* Jeremiah put the thought aside to enjoy the tight hug he was being given.

"Thank you so much for saving us," Jess said with her eyes wide and sparkling.

"I was worried about you Jess. What are friends for?" For some strange reason at that very moment Jeremiah wanted to be more than friends with Jess. At this moment he wanted to grasp her into his arms and tell her she would always be safe. When he looked back at her eyes they weren't nearly as bright. As if her feelings were hurt. "What's wrong? Aren't you happy to see me?"

"Of course I am," she said almost forcing a smile.

Her sadness suddenly seemed to fade away and her face shone with happiness.

"Let's get out of this rain or we'll both get sick."

"Smart thinking," Jeremiah grabbed his horse's reins and tied him next to Faith. "There you are boy," He patted the horse's neck.

Jess opened the dry tent and led the way in. Truthfully, Jeremiah felt kind of uncomfortable sharing a tent with Jess. It wasn't proper.

"Umm....Maybe I should keep watch for any other animals and keep an eye on the horses."

"Nonsense," She replied, "I'm worried about them too, but I'd feel terrible if you were up all night in that dreadful weather."

"Well, ok." He said nervously. Why am I so nervous? I'm never nervous around Jess. We're best friends, nothing more, even if I want more. "I don't feel comfortable about this," he blurted out.

"With what?"

Jeremiah gave her a knowing look.

"Oh.... about the tent." She whispered.

Even in the darkness Jeremiah could see her blush.

"We could just sit up and sleep," she suggested.

"Well, ok."

Jeremiah could feel the shivers up his spine as he sat in the darkness in the corner of the tent. He knew if they sat together they'd be warmer, because they could share body heat. "Are you cold?"

"Yes, very, I only brought one blanket."

"You keep it."

"You sure?"

"Positive."

She wrapped the cover around herself, but he could still hear her teeth chatter quietly.

"Listen, this is going to sound awkward but we're going to have to sit close to each other for body warmth."

"Can't disagree with you there."

Jeremiah scooted next to the warmth of Jess and she draped the cover over both of them. They snuggled closer and it was even warmer. Jeremiah could smell Jess' strawberry shampoo and feel her breath on his face. Before he knew it he was listening to her soft steady breathing. She was asleep. Jeremiah shut his eyes and in an instant he was asleep too.

CHAPTER 8 MY BATTLE WITH GOD

I woke up just in time to see the sun rising through the tent. I looked at Jeremiah. Somehow through the night he'd managed to get his arm around my waist. At that moment I realized that my head was on his shoulder. His head rested on mine. I breathed in his sweet aroma of damp hair and listened to his steady breath. *When he said, "What are friends for?" did he really mean we were just friends. Right now she felt as if they were more. Look at us. We're practically cuddling!*

Jeremiah stirred. *He can't wake up now. I'm enjoying this! I'll be so embarrassed if he wakes up and sees us in this position.*

Jeremiah blinked, then opened his eyes and gazed at me sleepily. His eyes grew wide once he fully woke up and saw how they looked together. "Umm...I'm sorry," he mumbled while his face turned redder than a ripe tomato. He swiftly drew his arm away from my waist. I soon missed the warmth.

I turned away. I couldn't look at him, for if I did I would surely blurt out what was truly on my mind.

"You ok?" he lifted my face with two large fingers and gazed at me as if he were searching for something.

I couldn't tell him; he'd only reject me.

"Well, I'm waiting?" He nudged my shoulder sweetly.

"I don't want to talk about it," I said forcing a smile.

"I do and we have all the time in the world, so cough it up,"

I could feel the heat crawl up my face. "Well, I'm really worried about Dad,"

"Are you sure that's it?"

I shrugged. "Can we talk about this later, after we eat, cause I'm starving,"

"Aren't you always? And yes, I guess we can."

Jeremiah crawled out of the tent and began to prepare breakfast while I followed and begin taking down our small camp.

Once we finished our silent meal Jeremiah cleared his throat, "You ready to head on home?"

I glared at him, "You should know by now that I'm not going home until I've searched in every nook and cranny to find my dad."

He looked deeply into my eyes. "Well, I'm not about to leave you in the wilderness all by yourself without a gun."

A smile spread across my face and impetuously I grabbed his neck in a bear hug, "Thank you so much. You have no idea what that means to me."

He smirked, "You're lucky I'm so nice."

"Yes, I am, Jeremiah. Yes, I am."

As Jeremiah unhitched the horses he smiled to himself. He couldn't believe the predicament he was in this morning. He awoke with a gorgeous girl eyeballing him as if he were a god! He chuckled to himself, but quickly stopped. He had felt so awkward when he had awakened. Jess's blonde hair falling onto her shoulders and her sparkling, blue eyes staring at him would make any guy uneasy.

"Jeremiah?"

"Yeah?"

"Will you help me put this tent back into its bag? I can't stuff it in here."

He grinned. "Sure." Jeremiah easily stuffed the oversized tent into its puny sac.

"Thank you," Jess said.

"No prob. Are you about ready to go on the search?"

Jess threw her leg effortlessly over Faith's saddle and smiled, "Now I am,"

"Alright. Let's go,"

They rode in silence for what seemed like an eternity. "You can tell me what's on your mind now," Jeremiah persuaded.

"I'd rather not,"

"Why?"

Jess turned away unable to look at him.

"Is it something that bad?"

"No," She mumbled.

"Well spit it out,"

"I kind of like someone,"

Hope welled in Jeremiah's chest. Why would I want her to like me? We are only friends. And yet for some reason I want more? "Who?" Jeremiah spoke softly.

Jess blushed. "I'll tell you later,"

No!! I can't wait till later. For some strange reason, Jeremiah felt that Alexis Bean just wasn't right for him. He desperately wanted Jess to be in his arms. "We have all the time in the world since we're just riding along,"

She inhaled a deep breath. "I'll tell you during lunch,"

Jeremiah felt defeated. Lunch was still a good two hours away. *How will I wait that long? I wish I'd never brought it up.*

I wish I would just drop dead! Jeremiah keeps pressuring me to reveal my feelings for him and Dad is nowhere in sight! This has to be the worst day ever! And I was dumb enough to promise him I would tell him. Now here we are setting up for our lunch under a colossal shade tree. Any minute now he'll bring it up.

"Who do you like?" He sought to know after we had said our prayer.

I sighed and gulped up a deep breath. "You," I murmured.

"What did you say?" He said with his eyes glued on me as though he thought I was lying.

"You," I repeated loudly. I turned the other direction **fighting embarrassed, unshed tears.**

He turned my head so I was facing him. "I've always liked you, but I've always thought you only **thought of me** as a friend."

I choked on my own air. I was in disbelief. "I thought you liked Alexis," I grunted.

"Well, lately I've been having mixed feelings for someone else," Jeremiah wiggled his eyebrows and **revealed a set of pearly white teeth in a flirty half grin. He gazed at me with his warm brown eyes and I practically collapsed in his arms.**

I swallowed the lump in my throat as the wind began blowing rapidly. "I've always had a special place in my **heart** for you."

He shyly **snuggled against me in a comforting fashion.** "We probably should eat our food before it gets cold."

"Yeah,"

We **enjoyed our meal together chatting happily when Jeremiah brought God up.**

"I think if we don't find your dad maybe it was his time to go. God's ways aren't our ways. He takes and gives."

Anger welled in my chest. If God's so great, why did He take Dad away from me!?! I think Jeremiah knows nothing. This is all God's fault!!

"You ok, Jess? You look kind of thoughtful there."

"I'm thoughtful alright." I growled.

"What's wrong? You were fine just a minute ago?"

"This is all God's fault and you know it! Why can't he just leave my life alone?"

"It's because God loves you. It says in John 3:16, For God so loved the world that he gave his only begotten son, that whosoever believeth in him shall not perish but have everlasting life. The verse means...."

"I don't care what it means, Jeremiah!! I never understand that thou art stuff, and you know it!! I don't know how you comprehend that garbage!" I boldly interrupted him.

"You need to know what it means."

"Maybe I don't want to hear it, because he's never helped me before."

"You know that was a lie a soon as you said it Jess. He's blessed you with innumerable things like **intelligence, beauty, a family that loves you, a normal** body, and so much more I can't count. The verse means **God loved you so much he let his only son get crucified on the cross so we could have the chance to have everlasting** life."

"Well, I still don't under**stand it; it makes no sense.** And now he's taking my dad away from my clutches and he expects me to forgive him?" Fuming tears started to **spill over onto my cheeks.**

"Yes, he didn't have...."

"Listen, Jeremiah, I've always liked you more than you'll ever know, but this won't work. We can't argue this same conversation every time I see you." Sobs were **choking out of my dry, hot throat. "I really like you, but** I've always thought you were too religious." Tears began **to flow and Jeremiah stared at me with bewilderment all over his face.**

"Maybe you can change."

"I can't change, and I don't want to have to change you." I'm never going to be good for Jeremiah. He's perfect and happy. I'm not; I'm a wasteful project unable to be fixed and ashamed to be in his presence. I'm not good enough for him.

"Jess? Jess?" Did you hear my question?"

"What was the question again?"

"Why can't we forget about this conversation and move on for now?"

"We'd only be feeding each other false hope. It won't work between us. We'll bicker over this religious trash and get nowhere." I released a sigh. I peered at him with sad, lost eyes. "You have no idea how much this pains me."

"Or me. Why can't we try to work it out?" He pleaded, "We haven't even started dating. Think of all the time we could spend together.

That sounded quite appealing, but I shook my head to clear my thoughts. I stood and began clearing where we had just finished our lunch.

"Well?" He peered at me with confused, gloomy eyes. "Am I getting the silent treatment, or do you just never want to try to work through this bump in the road?"

I began to weep openly and intensely. "I've always liked you, but I'm afraid if I don't find Dad I'll never even consider your God's love."

"But you just have to pray."

I shook my head. "This conversation is over, Jeremiah." I put the extra supplies in my sack and hoisted it on Faith.

Jeremiah looked at me sadly. "I just want the best for you and for you to be happy."

This was the best for him; I knew it. I managed to give him a weak smile. "We must go now, we must."

Sarah Gillespie

CHAPTER 9 MY INNER STRUGGLE

Jeremiah was baffled. I thought this was going to work out. Jeremiah stroked Hercules as he and Jess continued to follow the river towards the empty, desolate plains. It was already 3:00 and Jess hadn't said a word since lunch.

Dear Lord,

I hope she's thinking about you, Lord. You've granted each and every one of us your amazing love and grace. Please be with Jess and help me be able to touch her through you. Amen.

"Well, what are you thinking?" Jeremiah found the courage to ask.

"Nothing." She squeaked from her spot on top of Faith.

"I really do like you Jess. Even if we don't find your dad I'm always going to care about you just the same." He reached out his bulky hand and squeezed her delicate arm.

Jess didn't look at him. Her eyes weren't as sparkly as usual, and she acted as though every word she said was too much effort. "I...I...j..ust don't know." She wept quietly and struggled to gain control to speak.

She stared at him. Then he stopped her horse by pulling on the reins and surveyed Jess with intense eyes. He grabbed hold of her hand while they remained on their horses. Jeremiah slowly leaned toward Jess. Looking quite perplexed, she didn't make any struggle to stop him from moving toward her.

He guided the horses so they were touching one another. Then he gently took her into his arms.

She gazed at him closely and before he knew it he was enjoying the softest and sweetest kiss of his life. She placed her hands on his unshaven face while he placed his in her soft, warm hair.

"Did you change your mind?" He **murmured**.

She smiled. She leaned near his ear and whispered, "We'll just have to wait and see."

Hope welled in Jeremiah's soul. This has to work out. **Without thinking he began looking her up and down. Self-consciously he looked away with embarrassment. He knew without seeing himself that his face was on fire.**

Satisfaction soared through his heart. She had such soft, blue eyes, silky, smooth, blonde hair, and the cutest freckles speckled her face.

When he looked in her face, her sparkling eyes were fixed on him.

He bounded off his horse and effortlessly lifted her off hers.

He leaned down, wrapped his arms around her waist, and bent over so close he could feel her warm, steady breath. "What do you say now?"

She tilted his head back with her tender hands and angelically looked up into his eyes. She stood on her tiptoes to reach his tall stature. Then once again they shared an amazing kiss.

When the kiss was finally over he glanced at her and said, "Please say yes."

"How can I say no to that?"

His smile widened. He linked his fingers with hers and they walked back to the horses. He gently lifted her up on top of Faith.

"You're very special, Jessica Dean." He leaned so close to her mouth he could see every freckle in detail on her face.

Tears sprang into her eyes. "I've admired you since you stood up for me in the first grade."

Jeremiah reflected back to a time when things had seemed easier:

"Leave me alone!!" Jess wailed.

"Jess has old people glasses!" Jimmy hollered.

"Yeah, they look like you stole'm off me granny. And her mom don't know how to buy her any pretty clothes neither!" Alexis snorted.

"Leave me alone!!" Jess tried to act tough and strong but you could tell she was very weak in her spirits.

"My mommy says looks are what make a person. And you ain't got none so guess you're out of luck!" Alexis was high- fiving her small clan of friends.

Jeremiah came out from the small crowd that had gathered, "You're not ugly, Jess." He leaned real close to Jess and whispered, "Alexis is real ugly inside."

Jess smiled, "You're a true friend, Jeremiah."

Jeremiah draped his arm over her shoulder, "You too, Jess, you too."

Jeremiah focused on the present and thought, "Why was I even attracted to Alexis anyway? Jess is way more attractive inside and out. I must have forgotten how hateful she truly can act."

He leisurely walked to his horse and whispered in its ear, "I'm the luckiest guy to ever live on the planet. Don't ever let me give her up."

The stallion neighed in response.

"Yeah, I don't think I will either, even if I do need to work on her spirit."

I snuck a glance at Jeremiah as I continued to ride on Faith. He smiled that heart melting smile at me. I returned it with what I hoped was one of mine. *Why do I feel like this?* I feel like my heart has burst into a million pieces and has flown into the heavens. I feel as if I could leap into Jeremiah's arms and feel safe in his embrace.

"Jess?"

"Yes?"

"I've never felt like this before."

I looked away. I can't do this. He is way too sweet and good for me.

"Jess? Did you hear me?"

"Yeah," I leaned on Faith for comfort, "I've always wanted this, but I think you're....." I searched for the right words. My eyes stung and I turned away.

"What's wrong? I'm what?"

"Never mind. Dad!!! DAD!!!" My throat stung something awful. I screamed into the heavens to cover what I truly felt.

Jeremiah grabbed hold of my hand and smiled his charming half grin.

"I'm fine."

"O.k." He winked at me.

"Let's look for Dad. We've just reached this small patch of plains, and I really want to keep on task. DAADD!!!!!"

Jeremiah and I searched in every ditch and hole all through the plains for Dad, but he was nowhere to be found. I dug my face into my hands and bawled for everything I was worth.

"Dad, where are you?!" I wailed.

At that point Jeremiah had wrapped his muscular arms around me, "It'll be ok Jess."

He continued to hold me and baby me until the tears were no more. I'd cried all the tears out.
"Thanks," I muttered.

"You, alright?"

"Yeah, I'll be fine," I knew as soon as I said those words they weren't true. No, I was not ok. I was attracted to Jeremiah but, he could never want someone like me. I wasn't worth anything. He deserves someone more clever and Christian than me.

"You don't look fine to me,"

Jeremiah knew me too well. It's as if he can read me better than I can read myself. "I'll be all right." I commented in an exasperating tone.

He gave me an observant look.

I jutted out my lower lip and stared back. "I'll be o.k." I growled in an infuriating tone of voice.

"I'm just concerned." He flew back at me.

I let my eyes sink to my clutched hands holding Faith's reins. "I'm sorry for acting so rudely."

His face immediately softened. "I wasn't mad. I was more worried and unsettled about that gloomy frown taking over your pretty face."

He's way too kind for me! Why must he like me!! I wish this stupid God of his wouldn't have allowed this to happen to Dad! I wish Dad were here; he would know exactly what to say. He would tell me if Jeremiah was truly right for me or not. One thing was for sure, Dad was missing when I'd needed him most.

Sarah Gillespie

CHAPTER 10 DESTINY'S TRUE DESTINY

Jeremiah sat upon Hercules as Jess and he began to leave the plains. As the wind rustled the trees, he felt as though he could feel the Lord's presence. With all of God's nature surrounding him, he couldn't help but be reminded of Psalm 19. He looked at the world surrounding him. The Lord was amazing. He watched as the grass seemed to dance in the breeze. Then the wind picked up causing some loose leaves to twirl around Jess and him. He closed his eyes while he thought of his Lord. *Why was Jess so hard toward God? Why'd she have such a cold shoulder toward God?*

Dear Lord,

Please lift up Jessica. Give me the courage and strength to reach out to her. She is such a hard egg to crack. Please be with us so we may be safe on our travel, and, if it's your will, please Jesus, let us find her father.

Amen

Jeremiah opened his eyes as he concluded his prayer. He stroked the soft horse he was seated on.

"Jess?"

"Uhhhuh?"

"Will you please give God a chance to change your heart?"

Jess softly sighed, "NO."

Jeremiah had been licked, again. How was he ever going to get through to her? "Please?" Jeremiah looked at her with what he hoped was a very longing glance.

"I'll think about it."

"Yes! Maybe I will get through to her." Jeremiah rejoiced mentally.

"Listen. Right now I could care less about God. All I want is to find Dad and go back to my same simple, boring life."

"Your life's not boring."

Jess continued to look forward as though she didn't want to speak any longer.

Jeremiah glanced up into the sky. The sun was beginning to go down behind a patch of woods. "We should probably stop for the night and eat dinner."

"I suppose you're right." Jess gracefully hopped off Faith, and led her to a branch on a scarlet red maple tree.

Jeremiah began to climb off of Hercules when all of a sudden, in one quick motion, he started to lean to his left off the horse's saddle. Before he knew it, he was on the ground, embarrassed and stunned.

Jess began laughing hysterically as though he'd just finished the perfect prank.

"It's not that funny is it?" He questioned tauntingly.

Jess's head bobbled up and down while she pointed to something beneath him.

Jeremiah's eyes traveled from her bright smile to his back side on the ground. His face stung all the way to his ears. He had landed in a fresh pile of gooey horse manure. "Ahh, man! I don't remember if I brought any extra jeans!"

"Ha! Well, I guess Faith and I will just have to leave you here." She giggled, "We will have no smelly explorers on this trip!" Jess teased, her eyes filled with glee and making Jeremiah's stomach turn flip flops.

"Well, then, so the pile you're standing in doesn't count."

Jess leaned her head over. "Rats! No, it does not! Feet don't count in my book!" She said pretending to be boastful.

"Well, in my book, whatever book this is, it includes feet."

She laughed so hard he was afraid her face would turn blue, and she'd tumble over.

Jeremiah joined in the merriment and roared for all he was worth.

Jess was supporting herself against a tree as their laughter softened to chuckles and giggles. "Who's cleaning up first?" She managed to squeeze in between her high spirited fun.

"Lady's first." He replied in a mannerly tone, while leaning over extending his hands toward the river.

"Why thank you kind sir," Jess placed her soft palm in his hand before he gingerly kissed the top of it.

"Would the miss mind if she had a little company?" He whispered as they eyeballed each other.

"Why of course not kind sir."

"Thank you Lady, the kind sir is much obliged."

Jess began to move her delicate hand, but Jeremiah's fingers wouldn't let go.

She stared into his eyes as though he contained all the answers.

"Please don't let go," Jeremiah pleaded quietly, "I don't want to ever lose you."

"Likewise." She responded.

Jeremiah felt as if he'd just won a million dollars. He held her hand tightly indicating he never wanted to let go of it. "Well, beautiful Lady, what shall we have for dinner, beans or soup?"

"Definitely soup,"

"I think I must agree," He risked placing his arm around her waist, and shockingly she seemed at ease with the gesture.

Once they reached the river, it was time for them to clean up.

"Man, I really do stink!"

"You're not kidding," Jess snickered.

"You can go clean up first since yours is an easy, fast clean up,"

"Sounds good to me,"

Jess inched her way to the water's edge and slipped her boot off. She dipped the aged boot in the water and wiped the manure off into the grass. About five minutes later she was finished with the shoe, and it looked dazzling in comparison to the other one.

"Your turn," She proclaimed.

"Well…. Um…how should we do this?" Jeremiah made a circle in the dirt with the tip of his boot.

"Did you check to see if you had any extra jeans?"

"Darn! No, I forgot!" Jeremiah **massaged his head**, "I'm not about to have you walk all the way back to camp by yourself."

"How about if I turn the other direction?"

"That sounds good, but what do I do once I'm finished and I have no pants to put on until these dry?" Jeremiah **motioned to the denims he wore that contained an appalling stench.**

"Hmmm….." Jess came across some a plant with huge leaves. **Its leaves were about 36 inches long that were a frost**y-blue and green color. "I guess you could put one of those in front of you to cover your wet boxers and I'll walk in front of you a few yards away." She suggested.

"Well, I suppose that's all we can do," Jeremiah **rushed to the river and instructed Jess to turn the other** way, "No peeking," He hollered from the shore in a **serious tone of** voice.

"Ok," She answered once she turned her back.

This was probably going to be one of the most humiliating positions he'd ever been in, and he didn't like **it.**

I couldn't help but laugh at the predicament I was in with Jeremiah.

"Stop laughing at me," He ordered with snorts in-between each word.

"I can't help it!" I hooted. It felt kind of awkward to think I could turn around any moment and see Jeremiah in his underclothes. "Are you almost done?"

"Be patient, and yes I just have to get my leaf."
I snickered.

"Ha-ha, very funny. It wouldn't be so funny if it were you."

I hushed my giggles. He was right, as usual. I would be mortified if I were in his position. "Sorry,"

"It's ok," I could feel his presence behind me, "Just walk and don't even think about looking."

"Alright," I began walking back to camp about 100 yards away.

After an eternity went by, we finally arrived at our pathetic camp site. It was made up of two horses and a small glowing fire. The fire sparkled as golden colors and puffs of smoke ascended toward the sky. My mouth watered as I pictured myself roasting gooey, sticky marshmallows. It's too bad I didn't pack any.

"Don't look," Jeremiah demanded as he began to rummage through his backpack full of supplies.

"I already promised I wouldn't," I stated exasperatedly.

"Ok, good," He snickered, "I would have never guessed I would ever be in this kind of dilemma in my life."

"I don't think anyone means for these kinds of things to happen."

"Yeah," He grumbled.

I could hear Jeremiah digging and tossing as though he was sick of the strange circumstance he was in. "You don't have to hurry. I promised I wouldn't look,"

"I just really want my pants on,"

I chuckled. "I guess I can understand that,"

"Yes! I found some. Ok, I'm safe to look at now,"

"Finally! I felt like I was going to have to look into the woods forever." I turned around and admired him. He looked astonishing! His flannel, checkered shirt made him appear more masculine and made his brown eyes pop.

"What?"

I didn't realize my mouth had been gaping open. I shook my head, "Nothing."

"Do I really look that great?" Jeremiah asked.

"Yes!" I proclaimed mentally. "No, you hurt my eyes!" I said aloud as I smirked.

"Ha-ha very funny," He said as he hung his pants on a tree.

"We should probably head to bed," I suggested.

"Yeah, we don't have time to make the tent, so we'll just sleep against the horses next to the fire."

"Sounds good to me," I agreed.

After I was snuggled into my cover, I watched Jeremiah feed the fire a couple sticks. Before I knew it, the fire was blazing, warming my entire front side. I was thankful Faith was behind me or my back side would be freezing.

"I'm not tired," Jeremiah whispered disrupting my thoughts.

"Me neither," I shuddered as the wind picked up and blew against my face. In the light from the fire, I could see Jeremiah had a beard beginning to grow on his chin. Even in the darkness I could see his blonde stubble. He looked so handsome through the fire and in moonlight. I dared to peek into his eyes. He was looking at me intently. I quickly looked away, and when I snuck a glance back into his eyes, they were still glued on me

"You're....um....you...are....uh...never mind," Jeremiah stumbled over his words.

"I'm what?"

"Nothing," Jeremiah mumbled angrily. He rotated his head toward the stars. He looked as though he'd just been defeated.

I shut my eyes wondering what it would be like if I were a Christian or if Jeremiah weren't a Christian. Would we have a chance together? Do we have a chance now? I turned my body facing Faith. I dug my face into her neck. I breathed in her delicious aroma. Before I knew it I began to doze off into comforting slumber.

Destiny Taylor lay weeping on her kitchen table. "I hate my life!" She wailed, "First I lose my husband and now I can't find my baby!" She drew in a shaky breath.

"I wonder if Danielle was right about that praying thing. How could a God be lurking around me if I can't even see him?" Destiny wailed, "All I want is to find my family!"

At that moment the telephone rang. *Ring! Ring!*

"Hello," She sniffed.

"Hey," Danielle said in a soothing tone.

"Hi," Destiny grumbled.

"Listen, we're having a church service tonight if you want to come?"

"At 7:00 o'clock?"

"Yeah, we're having a summer night revival. Please, I think it will help you get your mind off the fact that the search team had a cancellation and still couldn't find them after we looked. The Lord is with my Jeremiah. I just know it. I know God is watching him." Danielle said confidently but sadness still lingered in her voice.

"Well, I guess it will get me out of the house."

"Good, we'll pick you up in five or ten minutes."

"Ok," Destiny rushed upstairs and threw on a pair of tan dress pants. Then she pulled on an orange blouse with yellow flowers embroidered on it. She glanced in the mirror and tousled her hair. She slipped on an aged pair of tan clogs, grabbed her purse, and headed to the porch.

As soon as she placed her foot on the porch Danielle and her husband, Brian, arrived in their green pick-up truck. "Ready?" Danielle called.

133

"Ready as I'll ever be," Destiny answered. She trudged to the truck and crawled into the crisp, clean back seat. She knew her good friend must be troubled. She only cleaned this well when she was upset.

Once they reached the church, Destiny was shaking from her nerves. "I shouldn't have come," She mentally moaned to herself.

Danielle grabbed her hand, "It'll be ok. Just think of it as being here for Christmas." She squeezed her hand gently and smiled weakly.

"It's not that easy."

"Sure it is," Danielle put her arm around her back in a reassuring fashion, "Trust me."

"Alright,"

After they took their seats, Destiny's mind told her to sprint home, but her legs didn't seem to work. She felt like her feet were bolted to the ground.

"Turn to page 81 in your hymnals," The preacher announced.

Destiny picked up her hymn and flipped through the pages. *'The Church in the Wildwood'* the page read back to her. She stuck her nose inside the book and began singing, "Oh, come, come, come," She glanced at her loyal friends. The couple weren't even using the books and didn't miss a single word! Those strange Christians always seemed perfect.

Everyone sang several more hymns and then the preacher began to preach.

He began to speak about a man named Job. This man had everything, wealth, livestock, servants, and family, everything he could dream of all because God gave it to him. One day Satan came to the Lord and said that he believed if Job lost everything he would turn against God. God disagreed, so Satan took away everything Job owned.

First a messenger came to Job and told him, Sabeans had stolen all his oxen, murdered his servants, and that he was the only one to survive. Then a second man came and said, a fire has fallen from heaven, destroyed all of his sheep and his servants, and he was the only one to survive. A third messenger arrived and told Job, the Chaldeans stole his camels, slayed all his servants, and he was the only one to survive. Then a fourth man came and told Job, his sons and daughters were feasting at their oldest brother's house, when a great wind blew and struck all four corners of the house and it collapsed on them, and he was the only one to survive. Job then tore his robe into pieces, shaved his head, and worshiped the Lord.

The preacher looked up after he'd finished reading out of Job Chapter 1.

"If Job can have that much faith, why can't we?" He questioned, "If you had just lost all of your possessions and more, would you worship God or blame God?"

Destiny sucked in a quick breath. She felt as though the sermon was designated for her. She felt as though she should have some faith her child and husband may return, if Job could still have that much faith through that tragedy. She felt as though the preacher was glaring at her as if to say, "Why do you shun God?" Destiny gulped in a large amount of air. He continued to say that we need Jesus through all our trials, small or big. That he was only a pray away and was a friend who would never leave you.

Once the preacher finished the service, Destiny couldn't hold back the tears any longer. They began spilling over by the gallons. As the church echoed *'Amazing Grace'* she began to make her way toward the alter in front of the church. Her mind begged to return to the security of her back row pew, but her legs kept moving. All eyes were in her direction, but for some strange reason she didn't care. Her legs felt as jello and as if any moment she would melt to the ground.

Finally she reached the alter and collapsed against it. Her vision was blurred by all the tears as she sat trembling. Seconds later a hand was placed upon her back.

"Do you want to know the Lord Jesus as your Savior?"

It took all Destiny's effort to nod.

"Do you believe our Lord Jesus died on the cross for all your sins and mistakes?"

She nodded vigorously.

"Do you want him to forgive you for all your sins?"

Again, she nodded.

"Ask him." He whispered tenderly.

Taking in a shaky breath she began, "Jesus. Lord, um.....pl..ease...forgive me for all of.... the sins I...I have...done wrong in your eyes. Amen."

The preacher rubbed her back in a brotherly manner and whispered, "Stay as long as you need to."

Destiny wiped her eyes as she stood up, "Is that all I have to do?"

He nodded, "Sure is. God has blessed us by forgiving us of all our wrong doing."

She grabbed him in an exuberant hug.

For the first time in months, Destiny felt at peace.

Jeremiah laid awake staring at Jess. *"Why am I attracted to her?"* He asked himself mentally. He'd felt so ignorant when he'd tried to tell her how gorgeous she looked before she fell asleep. Her eyes glowing in the sparkling fire light, her hair gleaming over her shoulder, she had been mesmerizing. She had looked as though she had just come down out of heaven in the form of an angel. It took all his effort to look at the stars, which were worthless in comparison. She looked so peaceful as she slept. She even seemed to smile in her slumber as if she were having a wonderful dream. Jeremiah could hear her steady breath from across the fire. The way she looked and sounded made him want to grab her into his arms. Jeremiah settled into his blanket for warmth. Try not to think about her. Maybe it will be easier to talk to her as we continue on the journey. Jeremiah forced his eyes closed as he told himself to sleep. He soon fell into an uneasy, restless sleep.

Sarah Gillespie

CHAPTER 11 SNEAKING OUT

The light shone brightly on my face as the sun came up. I rubbed my eyes drowsily with my sweaty, dirty palms. The fire was no longer a source of light or beauty. It was now a pile of glowing orange coals with gray smoke swirling, ascending its way into the heavens. I glanced across the fire. Jeremiah was fast asleep curled close to his horse. My attention then changed to Faith. I turned around to face her. She wasn't on the ground where I had left her. The wind was blowing briskly and the air was quite chilly for a late summer morning. I wrapped my cover around my shoulders, while my teeth chattered. A few yards away, Faith stood happily munching on a patch of green grass.

I smiled. I stood up and tiptoed toward her, trying to not wake Jeremiah.

Crunch. Crunch. The ground was so noisy as I took every step. Jeremiah rustled. I shot a glimpse his way. His eye lids flew open the second I looked at him.

He smiled at me. I leisurely walked to him and knelt on my knees, "Good morning," I whispered.

Jeremiah smiled, " You look great this morning."

I could feel the warmth rush to my neck and creep up my face. I shook my head. I can't like him. We're not meant to be together. I just know this won't work! Or will it?

He emerged out of his nest and drew me into his arms. He squeezed me as though I were a teddy bear. He gazed into my eyes. I could feel myself beginning to melt into his arms. I placed my hands on his chest and gently pushed him away. He looked at me as though I'd just kicked him in the gut.

"I'm sorry," I said, not able to look into his eyes.

"What's wrong? Is it me? Am I not good enough?"

I shook my head as I kept my eyes on the ground watching an ant scurry across the earth.

"Then what is it?

"You're…..um…it's not you. I already told you."

"What about? Oh, church? It's ok…"

"No," I cut him off, "I don't want to change. And I don't think I can change you. And….." I traveled off and didn't finish my sentence.

"And what?" He asked.

"And nothing."

He gave me a knowingly look.

"I think I'm, you're, oh nothing," I kept my eyes on the dirt beneath me. I grabbed a leaf and began to crumble it between my fingers.

"Well are you going to tell me?"

"I can't." I said. I rubbed my arms pretending I had a cold chill and began to stand up. I rushed toward Faith before he had time to reply. I did not want to tell him I wasn't good enough for him. Rejection would only be harder to swallow.

He followed me whether I wanted him to or not. I truly wished he had not.

"Get your horse hitched and let's go," He grumbled in an infuriated tone of voice.

"Ok, but,"

"But nothing,"

He hitched his horse and was on in him in a flash. I did the same.

I did not like where this was going, not one bit.

Jeremiah kept his eyes straight ahead. He refused to look at such beauty if she saw nothing in return. His heart ached to be with her, and embrace her in his arms.

"Listen, I'm sorry,"

"Don't waste your breath," He growled. Jeremiah shot a glance of her. She was perfect for him, at least so he thought. He looked up into the trees as they continued to ride. He spotted a blue jay chasing after his mate. 'Good luck.' He thought ruefully. If that bird's as lucky as me, he may as well chase a hawk.

Jeremiah and Jess continued to follow the river when they came upon Beaverhead Mountains. The mountains were immense and could take months to check.

"Maybe we should split up," I suggested.

"No,"

"Why, it'd be faster and…"

"No, I'm not going to leave you alone in the mountains."

"But…"

"No!" Jeremiah shot his eyes on the leaf covered ground, "I refuse it," he grumbled. No, way in this world would he ever leave her alone without any protection. NO WAY!

"Can't I at least explain my reasoning?" She looked at him with deep pity and longing.

"You may, but I won't change my mind and I won't listen," Jeremiah felt as though he was being harsh but he didn't want to risk it. Better be safe than sorry.

She tried to clarify her reasoning to him but Jeremiah rebuffed her.

"Please,"

Jeremiah began to ignore her. He drew his attention to a small chipmunk scurrying across the earth searching for any shelter.

The sun was slowly coming down in the west.

"We'd best make fire," Jeremiah ordered.

Jess didn't respond.

Jeremiah hopped off his horse and began to prepare camp. Jess didn't budge off of Faith.

"Well, are you going to come down?" Jeremiah inquired.

Jess avoided eye contact by glaring into the forest. "I'm going to look for him,"

'Well, if she wants to be stubborn so can I.' thought Jeremiah as he glared at her. If she won't move I won't sleep.

"No, you're not!" He bellowed.

Soon, it grew dark and the only light source was the fire and the full moon hiding behind the clouds.

Jess still sat on the horse, while Jeremiah lay next to the fire cradling his rifle.

"I'm not sleeping," He protested.

"Me either," She hissed back.

Jeremiah rustled on the ground in a more comfortable position. He threw the blanket around him and stared at the golden, warm light. Jess still had her eyes glued on the forest, showing no fear in it, whatsoever. Jeremiah's eyes commenced to close. He jerked them awake, knowing he had to watch Jess. He knew her stubbornness would get the better of her and she would go. His eye lids started to feel as heavy as cement and before he knew it, he was asleep.

I glanced over my shoulder to see if he was still awake. Yes!! He was out. I guided Faith to face Jeremiah.

"Told you I'd go anyway," I whispered. I turned Faith toward the woods and was off in a heartbeat. I rode in the darkness, with only the moon as my light. It glistened through the tree tops on the forest floor. In the shadows I could not even see Faith's mane before me. I put her into a canter. I was beginning to get anxious, since I knew I needed to find dad.

I felt as though the trees surrounded me, making me feel claustrophobic. I imagined glowing yellow eyes staring at me as though I were some freak, as if I were out of place in the woods. I pet Faith's mane for courage and strength. I closed my eyes pretending this was still a dream. The wind howled bringing my eyes open again to see nothing but darkness. I shivered in the loneliness and solitude the wind brought as it came and went. I shut my eyes again hoping to reminisce on Jeremiah.

I dreamt that Jeremiah and I would someday be together in harmony. That it all really would work out. Maybe we'd get married and have beautiful children. We'd live happily ever after, like a book. I reopened my eyes focusing on the ground since there was no trail. The ground was harsh, rough, and as dark as a chunk of coal, but I persisted on the journey.

The owls hooted in the distance searching for prey. The wind whistled causing the air to feel as though there were a tribe of Indians in my presence. The trees teetered back and forth dancing in the gust of air, tempting rain to come at any moment. The crickets played a melody searching for their mates.

I put Faith into a gallop forcing her to go as fast as she could over the logs, brush, and limp, baby trees.

I leaned down into her ear and murmured, "Thanks girl for always being there for me." I patted her pleasantly. She was all I had left.

I soon stopped since I could tell Faith was tired and needed a break from exhaustion. I quickly looked at my watch. It was 1:00 A.M., so I decided to make camp. Faith lay down in a small patch of itchy brush, so I

Sarah Gillespie

impetuously knelt beside her and made my nest as well. I
curled in a little cocoon and was soon out cold.

CHAPTER 12 DAD'S WHITSLE

Jeremiah woke with a start. He had been having a petrifying dream. He was chasing Jess. She was screaming 'Help! Jeremiah!' He forced and strained with all his might but his legs wouldn't move. They felt as though they were bolted to the ground. He stretched his arms as far as he could reach but it was no use. She began fading in the distance. Jeremiah tried to tell her to stop and to wait but he was dumb. He couldn't say a word, or even make the simplest sound. Then she vanished, and here he was now coated in perspiration and out of breath.

He eased his head up slowly still in a daze. He looked over the campsite. No Jess or Faith. Jeremiah fell backward into his resting spot. 'What am I going to do now? No Jess or Faith. My own faith is beginning to wan.' He reflected in his thoughts. Jeremiah punched his small lifeless pillow, hoping to take out the anger he now contained, sadly it didn't work. Jeremiah sought Hercules eyes for all the hope, courage, and trust they contained. He turned around, but Hercules was no longer behind him.

"Here boy!" He hollered.

In an instant, his horse bounded from around the corner of a sea of trees.

"There you are boy," Jeremiah was now on his feet sprinting toward his beloved friend.

Once Jeremiah was with Hercules, he was off to find Jess. He mounted on his horse and kicked him into a canter.

"The pain a woman puts you through," Jeremiah lectured to Hercules, "You know what it's like? You go to chase after Faith, while she tempts you, but as soon as you're within 10 feet of her she sprints. I just wish Jess'd choose a side, like me or not. I don't think I can take much more of this, but Hercules she's the only one who seems to know me. We always have a common subject to talk about, except God. I just wish she could see God's love and what he truly has to offer. It's like she shuns and blames God for this tragedy we're enduring." Jeremiah patted his stallion, "Maybe this all happened for a reason? Who knows, I just wish God would tell me."

I awoke with a start at seven, ready to start my travels. I had no intension of letting Jeremiah catch up with me just to give me a long sermon about how we should stay together even though it wouldn't work. I sat up and stroked Faith behind her ear.

"Let's go girl," I encouraged.

She quickly arose and was ready for our journey. I leaped on her back and jabbed my ankles into her stomach. We were off.

"Dad!! Dad!!!" I paused, "Where are you?"

Beaverhead Mountains echoed my voice and returned it back to me. All I could hear was the soft trickles of the nearby creek. The leaves were rustling in the calm wind. The birds were humming sweet tunes merrily. I felt discouraged, but I continued onward with determination.

An hour went by and I came upon a small pond. I hopped off to stretch my legs. I allowed Faith to have a cool drink in the blue-green pool. I sat on a firm, solid rock to wait for Faith to finish.

I began to feel very disheartened. I had searched high and low for days and yet there had been no sign of him. I wiped a small tear that had made its way down my face. There was no hope for him, he was gone.

"Dad where are you?!!" I shouted out of anger and madness, "I've been very patient and still I don't hear you!" My vision was blurred immensely. The tears kept coming. I lifted my knees to my face and buried myself into my arms.

Then I heard a soft, high pitch noise. I hushed. There it was again. It sounded like a faint whistle in the distance. I grabbed my whistle from my first-aid kit and blew on it as loud as I could. Again I heard the soft whistle in response. I hopped on Faith, and forced her in a gallop.

"Go, girl, go," I commanded.

"Dad!!" I roared.

The whistle grew louder in the east. I turned Faith around and began to follow a small, trickling creek.

"DAD whistle again!!" Tears of happiness began dispensing heavily on my face.

The whistle was near. I shot off Faith and commenced my hunt for my father. I dug in the brush but I saw no sign of him. Then I noticed Faith walking in the woods. Behind the brush was Spirit. I ran to Faith to congratulate her for her finding Spirit, but something was amiss.

I ran to Spirit's side, with a sour expression on my face. I examined his body; he had been bitten by a snake and was gone. I heard a small whimper, "Dad," I whispered. Perspiration and tears was pouring off my face now.

"Help," cried the soft voice. In a deep pile of grass sat dad with a small fire. He was sitting close to the creek and was trying to swallow down a starwort plant.

"Dad," I whispered, "You're alive." I ran to his side and clung to his neck.

"Praise the Lord! I thought I was stranded here forever!"

"Praise the Lord? Dad what's your problem? You never say that. And how do you know it was God who saved you? I think it's a bunch of nonsense."

"Listen, I've been stuck here for quite some time. I began praying someone would come to my rescue. He answered my prayers, Sweetie. God is a blessing."

"But you never thought this before."

"I know, but that was before I realized how much I needed him. He was someone I could talk to. Someone I could ask for help and strength. He was gracious enough to give me those things."

"But it's God's fault you are in this mess!?"

"I think he had his reasons, because now I'm closer to him."

"Do you understand all that crucified stuff? You know, where he died on the cross for our sins. It all makes no sense."

"Well, I did understand it, but I didn't fully believe it. I didn't think anyone would die on a cross for the world's sins. But if it wasn't for Danielle giving me this Bible, I wouldn't have learned that. I had stuck it in my backpack and had forgotten about it. I was extremely bored while I was stranded out here and I began reading it. Now I have given myself to God and am a full hearted Christian."

"Oh, my gosh! I didn't ask you what was wrong!"

"It's nothing really. I hurt my ankle so I couldn't go anywhere for a long distance. I just made a splint and hoped for the best."

"But how'd it happen?"

"Well, it was your birthday and I was coming out here to find the perfect spot in the woods to have our picnic."

"But why so far?"

"I knew you'd want it to be further out to explore, but I wanted to examine the area first."

"Oh," I replied.

"Anyway, I came out here and Spirit saw the snake before I did. He got bit as I tried to calm him down, but it was too late. He fell hard on my right side. He got up as soon as he'd done the damage and limped away. He soon was gone."

I inspected his right side. His ankle was a deep purple and had a splint made from a tree branch. It was very swollen from the ankle all the way down to his toes. He had a couple bumps and bruises, but overall he seemed to be alright. "Your ankle doesn't look too good,"

"Yeah, don't believe there is any other damage. At least I hope not."

"Those idiotic search men. They searched for days! It's pathetic that a sixteen year old finds you, when they can't."

"Honey, calm down, this all had to happen for a reason."

"Well, if I hadn't found you, you'd be a goner for sure. I'm sure glad you didn't have any run ins with wild animals."

"Did you?"

"Well, I had an encounter with a mountain lion."

"Sweetie! Are you ok!?"

"I'm okay ."

"You didn't have a gun, what did you do?"

"Well, uh…..Jeremiah saved me."

"I always have liked that boy, and I have an **itching** you have to."

My face turned crimson. "Well, um….. uhh…"

"Ah, huh, I knew it. I knew you always liked him. **Now where is he anyway?**"

"Well, I ditched him,"

"What! Why? A boy risks his life for you and you ditch him?"

"Well, I wanted us to split up and he wouldn't hear of it. He said it wasn't safe and…"

"The boy was right. It isn't safe to split up and you know it." He said interrupting my sentence.

"I just wanted to find you as soon as possible."

"Ok, but you were left defenseless in the process. I thought you liked him, so why would you want to leave him?"

"Ummmm...... I think he could do better than me and we were fighting because he wanted me to believe in God. God's a phony. We're just lucky I found you before it was too late, no thanks to his God."

"Sweetie, let me explain something. God is an almighty God who loves us more than we will ever know. Here I'll read a verse, *John 3:16 For God so loved the world, that he gave his only begotten son, that whosoever believeth in him shall not perish but have everlasting life.*" He closed the Bible, "What it means is that God sent his only son to earth to die for all the people's sins, like stealing, murdering, envy. Everyone sins because no one's perfect. Since God sent his son, Jesus, he has given us the choice to either go to heaven or hell. By dying on the cross he has forgiven us for all our sins, proving that he is an almighty, merciful God."

"It's all starting to make sense, but how do I know he's real?"

"Well, God left us this Bible full of instructions. We just have to believe and have faith."

I gave him a look of bewilderment.

"I'll explain more later, we should begin our travel home, and find Jeremiah. Also, why do you think Jeremiah would save you from a mountain lion if he didn't care about you?"

I parted my lips to speak but no words would escape them.

"Yep, speechless. Your old man's not as dumb as he looks."

I clenched my dad's hand. "I'm so happy you're ok."

"Me too, sweetheart, me too."

Sarah Gillespie

CHAPTER 13 ALL BECAUSE OF FAITH

Jeremiah guided his horse to a small pond allowing Hercules to have a refreshing drink. He stroked him on the neck, for reassurance.

As soon as he was finished drinking, Jeremiah leaped on his back and was off on his search.

"Jess!!! Jess!!! Where are you?"

No answer, Jeremiah's hope was beginning to vanish. Then he heard two soft whistles from the east. He redirected Hercules' path and followed the high pitch. They soon grew louder.

"Hello, anyone there?!" He yelled.

"Dad, I hear him!"

There was Jess' voice.

"Jess?!"

"We're coming!"

Then out of the brush came Faith carrying Josh and Jess.

"You're ok! You are both ok!" Jeremiah smiled **revealing all of his pearly white teeth.**

"Yes we are ok." Jess sa**id moving Faith toward Jeremiah**, "The question is are you ok?"

"I'm perfectly fine now but I was petrified when I **awoke and** you were gone."

Josh gave Jess a knowingly look.

"What was that for?" Jeremiah wanted to know.

"Nothing," Josh smiled at Jess who happily returned the smile, "Well, we were looking for you, and now that we found you, we're gonna head on home."

"Oh, ok." Jeremiah nodded in agreement. He was still quite bewildered with the strange look Josh had given his daughter. It wasn't just any kind of look, more like an 'I told you so' look.

"Well, I think I'm going to go to the bathroom," announced Josh.

Jess hopped off Faith, letting her father take her horse to assist him to use the necessaries.

She walked toward Jeremiah in a leisurely fashion as though anticipating talking to him. "I'm sorry," She whispered.

"Why?" Jeremiah spoke softly in return as he slowly dismounted off his horse.

"For running away, not listening to you, ignoring and blaming God, and…"

Jeremiah was shocked speechless.

"And for not telling you how much you mean to me."

Jeremiah pulled Jess into his arms. "I've known you were special since I stood up for you at school. Do you understand God's will and what he has done for you?"

165

"Surprisingly yes, my father explained it to me and I asked God to forgive me of my sins and to come into my heart. I feel wonderful and free from all my troubles!"

Jeremiah refused to let go of Jess, "I've missed you; you make me so very happy, Jess."

"You make me happy too," She returned his hug tightly.

"Am I interrupting something?" Josh asked grinning, while the pair blushed.

"I knew you two were love birds,"

Jess giggled, "Well, we probably should go home and make our families' day."

"I suppose you're right," Josh grinned.

Destiny Taylor stood in her kitchen staring out her window. She was clutching her Bible for strength and courage. God had made her feel at peace and loved, yet she still felt emptiness inside. She knew what she was missing. Her dear husband and daughter were gone and she was beginning to lose hope. She sat down at the kitchen table and rested her head in her sweaty, shaky palms. She reached for the phone and dialed Danielle's number.

"Hello?" Asked a feminine voice.

"Hey, Danielle, why don't you and Brian come over for dinner?"

"Well, we'd be delighted. You ok?"

Destiny sniffed, "No,"

"I know, I miss'em too." She replied, "I've been worried sick."

"I just can't take it anymore. Every night I go to sleep in an empty bed, an empty house with no love. I….just…..I've been praying and praying."

"Sometimes God doesn't answer our prayers the way we want or think they should be answered."

Destiny agreed, "I suppose you are right."

"Now you go a make a surprise meal for us."

"Alright, see you soon."

In an hour Danielle had cooked steak and tossed salad and was setting the table when her two dear friends arrived.

"It smells delicious," Brian commented.

"It sure does," Danielle agreed.

"Thank you,"

Her two friends sat at the table as Destiny washed her hands. She took one last glance out the window, hoping to see her family walking towards her. She saw two horses with three figures mounted on top.

Destiny was astonished, speechless at that.

"Is something wrong?" asked Danielle.

Destiny slowly drew her pointer finger to the window, "They're.....They're here!!!!"

She dashed out the back door letting it slam behind her. She ran with all her might towards the figures, hearing the footsteps of her friends behind her.

"You're home!!!" She proclaimed joyously.

Jess hopped off her horse and ran to greet her. "I'm home mom!"

Destiny embraced her in a tight hug, "I love you."

"I love you too,"

Destiny took hold of her daughter's hand and rushed to her husband, "Josh," she whispered. She stretched up on her tiptoes and hugged her husband for all he was worth. "I'm so glad you two are ok."

By this point, the Foremen family had made their way toward the happy reunion.

Danielle announced, "You have no idea how much you have been worrying us."

"That's for sure." Destiny said with teary eyes.

"What happened?"

"It's a long story," Jeremiah smiled at Jess.

"Well, how'd you three do it?" Destiny wanted to know.

Jess stood next to her father who was mounted on her horse. She stroked the horse's neck and replied, "I guess all we needed was a little bit of Faith."

Sarah Gillespie

ABOUT THE AUTHOR

Sarah Gillespie is a sixteen year old student from West Virginia. She plays volleyball and lacrosse, while balancing her 4.28 grade point average. She also is a member of the Sand Run Baptist Church, 4-H and Fellowship of Christian Athletes. In her spare time she enjoys playing piano and spending time with her family and friends.

Feel free to contact me at my blog www.faithfullysarah.blogspot.com or e-mail me at faithfullysarah@yahoo.com. I would be honored to hear from my readers. Please send me feedback!

Sarah Gillespie